MESMERIZED

A SCI-FI SHORT STORY COLLECTION

JOHN P. WARREN

Copyright © 2024 John P. Warren

Layout design and Copyright © 2024 by Next Chapter

Published 2024 by Next Chapter

Cover art by Jaylord Bonnit

Large Print Edition

This book is a work of fiction. Names, characters, places, and incidents are the product of the author's imagination or are used fictitiously. Any resemblance to actual events, locales, or persons, living or dead, is purely coincidental.

All rights reserved. No part of this book may be reproduced or transmitted in any form or by any means, electronic or mechanical, including photocopying, recording, or by any information storage and retrieval system, without the author's permission.

WHEN DREAMS AND MIRAGES COLLIDE

They call me Zack Jauntly, and as my surname suggests, I really went on a strange, mind-altering journey. The day before all of this began, I was seated in a far corner of a silent bar, having a coffee with what I call my "agent."

I say to him, "I'm so depressed it hurts—my nervous system is in pain. It's like a clenched fist squeezing the life out of my heart. I've been in this job too long. It's killing me."

"That's the nature of our job. I'm afraid it comes with the territory. I need to know if your shop is still open and not how your demons are suddenly haunting you."

"Yeah, it's open. What have you got?"

The agent reaches down to his satchel, which is on the ground in a tidy, upright position, picks out a file, and hands it to me. "There, your next assignment, and no, it will not do much for your mental health."

I'm instinctively drawn to the picture of a man that's attached to the file by a paperclip. The picture is striking to me because I believe the man to be a mean-looking son of a bitch. "What's he done?" I ask.

"He was a crooked cop. He went after a pretty young woman and began harassing her husband when she rejected him. The husband since took his own life because of the pressure. He got off—the cop did, that is."

"I think I'm gonna enjoy taking this jerk out," I reply as I fold up the file and place it inside my jacket. I get up and leave the older man, who finishes his coffee.

Outside the bar, I look carefully around, scanning the vicinity for any hostile enemies lurking in shadows who may be seeking revenge for contracts I carried out in the past. The coast seems clear, and I continue to my old car, a beaten-up Corvette. I get inside and drive off. Later that evening, I am with my girlfriend in her bedroom at her apartment. Her name is Zoe. We were together intimately, and I light a cigarette. I gesture to Zoe to light up too. She pushes it away.

"I don't think that's a good idea now."

I laugh. "Why? Are you pregnant or something?"

"Yeah, I am."

I'm stunned. The next day, I am spying on the cop—my next contract. The cop gets inside his squad car and drives off. I presume he is heading for the police station on his way to work. I follow him. As we make our way downtown, the cop never notices that I'm following him. He pulls up beside a group of what seem to be drug dealers—they have unsavoury impressions of themselves, judging by their poor hygiene and attire. I park a respectful distance away, take out my binoculars from the glove box, and peer through them. I witness one of the gang members handing the cop a large envelope, probably a payoff so they can carry out their nefarious deeds. The cop takes the filthy cash, returns to his car, and drives off. I continue to follow him.

We are now both outside the police station, where I can see him picking up his phone to answer an incoming call. He drives away from the police station, never entering it at all. I presume this to be odd and believe he is on a case where something has come up. I remind myself that I am on a contract and have to carry it out, so I continue following him. The cop drives all the way out to a block of middle-class apartments and gets out. I remember that one of the cop's girlfriends lives there, so I quickly take out the file for the apartment number. The cop heads to the entrance of the apartment block, only to be subjected to a diatribe of abuse from a young woman. She is yelling and screaming at him. *Was he doing the same to this young woman as he was to the other couple that was the reason for his current contract?* I think to myself.

The cop makes a gesture with his hand, signalling that he can't listen to her complaints and heads back to his car. Realising that the coast is clear, and this is my opportunity to take him out, I pick up my revolver, which I keep well concealed in my coat, and point the weapon at the cop. I squeeze the trigger and fire, only the young woman comes out of nowhere. As the bullet impales her flesh, I dive into the murky depths of unforgiving despair. When I realise I've killed this woman, I throw the weapon into the back seat and speed off. As I try to escape, my driving is erratic, and the thoughts flooding through my mind are that I'm the bad guy now because I screwed up and broke the cardinal rule—no women and no children, only evil men.

Much later that evening, I hide in my cabin in the woods outside the city. I frantically pack a suitcase and delve through my stash of fake passports as I plan to leave the country by tonight. I head over to the drinks cabinet, take out a bottle of tequila, and gulp some of it down. I am sweating as it is a very humid evening, and I am hysterical with worry and fear. I look under my bed, pull out a can of gasoline, and douse the cabin. I leave the gasoline-saturated wooden cabin, light a match, and hurry to my car, carrying a small suitcase. The cabin goes up in flames suddenly. I can feel the heat emanating from the blaze. I get inside the car and drive off. As I make my way down the hill, the car starts to break down, so I slow down and get out, carrying the suitcase with me and the bottle of tequila. I know I'll have to sleep somewhere deep in the woods tonight and take my chances that nobody will find me.

Staggering and falling against the bushes and trees, I scare an owl and fall to the stony ground, unconscious. It is dawn, and as the sunlight dazzles my eyes just as I open them, I vomit.

"Are you alright, son?" a strange voice says, sounding as if it came from a Native American man.

I turn around and see it is a Native American elderly man dressed in a Chief's attire.

"My apologies for getting sick on your land."

"That's okay. I'm sure you can make amends for it somehow."

"Sure, no problem. I don't suppose you could tell me the quickest way out of here?"

"No doubt you're lost. I can help you rediscover your path."

"Yeah, that's right—a path outta here."

"The path I'm going to show you will take you on a journey that will enrich your soul."

I am agitated now because I'm very hungover and not having any of it. "For God's sake! Enough of the Indian mumbo jumbo—just show me the way out of this fucking forest!"

The Chief moves swiftly over to me and strikes me across the face. I am about to punch him back, but the Chief intercepts me and punches me instead.

"You listen here! I know the reasons for your predicament. You caused the death of an innocent woman!" the Chief yells.

"Are you here to take me out?"

"No, you fool. I'm here to make it all better."

"Just how in the hell are you gonna do that, Chief?"

"Oh, I don't know. Maybe I'll practise a little of that 'mumbo jumbo,' as you like to call it."

"Heaven knows it might help."

"Just stand back, and I'll show you."

I finish rubbing my face and stand back up. The Chief brings me a few yards to an area of cleared forest. There is a fire burning in the middle of the ground, surrounded by small rocks. The Chief takes from his pocket a vial of blue-coloured powder and pours it into the fire. There is a whoosh of flames followed by bluish smoke and a quivering effect seen through the small plume of smoke.

"What are you doing?" I ask him.

He casually replies, "—Just manipulating the fabric of space/time."

"What?!" I say, astonished and incredulous.

"The energy released from this vortex is literally handing you a gift. When you experience this gift, I want you to find me and tell me what you saw because maybe I'm right or maybe I'm so wrong."

"What?"

"I said fuck off now."

I don't wait around so the crazy bastard can do any more voodoo on me, so I run. It wasn't long before I found my car. I drive off. Paranoid that I am too late to flee the country, I head for my downtown apartment. It is on the opposite end of the city. It is quaint, and when I get there, I hit the bed and sleep. That night, I have a crazy dream of a thirteen-year-old girl who was living in my home with Zoe and calling me daddy. Then there was a knock on the door. I went to see who it was, naturally. When I opened the door and, to my horror, it was the Chief.

"You?!" I tried to utter, but I couldn't speak properly.

"It's time," he replied.

"Time for just what?"

"Depending on when you're getting this message, all this should be clear to you. However, because of what I performed on you during our first meeting in the forest, the timing could be unpredictable."

"What are you talking about, man?!" I screamed at him.

The Chief sighed. "To hand over *her*," he says, pointing at my daughter.

I knew that he wanted her for something no good, and at that moment the mere suggestion of handing over my flesh and blood to a person badder than I ever was wasn't something I could ever humanly do. I yelled at him to get out. I then grabbed the child and held on to her as long as I could, and as fear of losing her washed over me, I cried.

Waking up in my apartment, sweating profusely and very confused, *why was I so adamant about holding onto a child?* I decide not to think about it too much and get up to pour myself bourbon. The next day, I never leave the apartment. There is widespread revulsion being projected on the news reports of the murder of an innocent young woman that I am one hundred percent responsible for. I decide there and then to keep a low profile and do things like shopping for groceries online. I am basically housebound. I know that my so-called 'agent' is probably searching for me and, besides him, the police. I decide that I have to revise my original plan and try to flee the country or something else. This means calling up an old friend or more of a former colleague of mine.

I pull out my backup cell phone that I call my 'Master Phone' from underneath the floorboards. It has the numbers of my colleagues who I can trust. I scroll down the contacts list and find one. It is the number of a man ten years older than me and specialises in damage limitation, and heaven knows I need damage limitation right now. His name is Kevin McKenzie, and I immediately dial his number. There is the dial tone, and I am becoming increasingly anxious and agitated as it continues to sound with no pick-up from McKenzie. I'm about to fling the phone across the room when he picks up. "Jaunt, strange, it sure has been some time."

Breathing in a deep breath of stale air and wiping the cold sweat off my forehead, he annoys me. He always, like most of my acquaintances, calls me by the nickname 'Jaunt', short for Jauntly. "McKenzie, are you open?"

"I sure am. Where this time?"

"At my second home. You know the one, as you were there a few summers ago."

"Oh, that's right. I know it. I guess you wouldn't be calling if it weren't critical."

"Yeah, it's 'critical'."

"I'll be there in three hours from now."

"Good."

The phone line sounds like he hung up abruptly and curtly. I breathe a sigh of relief and decide I can eat. The last thing I need is to have a low blood sugar level crippling my thinking as I'm trying to explain and understand McKenzie's superfluous scientific methods of fixing problems. Last night's dream or nightmare is now a forgotten memory in my mind. Instead, the burning issue racing through my head is: *could I really trust Kevin McKenzie?*

After much introspective deliberation, I decide I haven't much of a choice. When I recall the times he had double-crossed me, even more than I care to remember, I shudder. I always slept with my revolver fully loaded and underneath the pillow next to me, so I guess I would have to be just as meticulous when I deal with him. He is a sloppy individual but a consummate professional. Maybe he believes that his unkempt image, that he likes to illustrate right down to his poor hygiene, gives the impression that he is nothing more than a bum, and it affords him some kind of reassurance that instils confidence in his own personal skills. I never saw it like that, and thinking along those lines instils confidence in him from myself and that he will do the job the right way.

Three hours pass, and I can see McKenzie's van pull up outside. He gets out and spits on the ground, then obliterates the vulgar evidence by rubbing his right shoe on it. He looks up at the rundown high-rise and smirks to himself. All this I can witness clearly as I'm located midway up.

He is insulted because he thinks everyone has a low opinion of him. I just don't give a fuck about what people think of me.

"Ok, Jaunt, you seem to be neck-deep. I have the solution, but first, I wanna see the dollars."

I search and drag a suitcase out from under the bed, take the key from my pocket and open it, displaying the cash. "Half your fee is there. The other half when you get me outta this sorry mess."

"Lovely," he says, counting the money. "Jaunt, you'll have nothing to worry about. I'm right on it. See ya in a month."

"A month?"

"For the other half of my fee."

"Just make sure you get me off the hook."

He leaves and good riddance. The fridge beckons me. Grabbing an ice-cold beer to ease my thirst and frustration, I hit the sofa, stretching my aching limbs. I fall asleep and begin dreaming of being in the same house where I was in the dream last night. Zoe is preparing dinner. She calls the little girl to come to the table, only a teenager comes down the stairs. The little girl in my previous dream is now much older, and come to think of it, Zoe has aged too. It sounded like she called our daughter 'Emma'.

We each head for the table. I don't know why I feel so hungry. Then Zoe asks, "How did work go?"

I reply, "Fine."

Have I gone straight? I must've done. Then Emma nudges me. "Daddy, will you help me out with the calculus? It's hard to understand."

"Sure. Maths is my speciality."

Zoe serves up a roast, and I absorb the aroma of a well-cooked home meal by my loving wife. The picture-perfect family scene is interrupted by the doorbell ringing. I immediately stop what I'm doing and head to the door to answer our visitor. I open the door, and it's none other than the Chief I first became acquainted with all those years ago when I screwed up my last assignment.

"You?!" I exclaim softly.

"Hello, Zack. It's time now. This is the end of your path. The path I put you on all those years ago."

"What do you want?" I ask.

"I—we—require your daughter."

I look him in his stony grey eyes and see no emotional empathy for me or my family. Then, I cast aside the strong feelings of losing my only child and become just as cold as he is. "I will get her at once." I say it as though I am devoid of even the merest human emotion towards my daughter, as if I am some kind of automaton.

I return to the living room and grab Emma. She is frightened and yells. When we arrive at our front door, I just hand her over to the Chief and then shut the door. I can hear her obvious screams and remain impervious to her plight, with a stagnating indifference. I wake up.

As earlier this morning, I am just as revulsed and self-loathing. I can't bring myself even to the mere contemplation of surrendering the daughter I had in my dreams. These feelings amaze me because, in reality, I was in the mindset of wanting nothing to do with Zoe's baby, even if it were mine. I am locked in a nexus of confusion and despair, like being pulled by the sombre gravitational forces of the worst emotions the macabre human psyche is capable of.

I am disguised and outside the front door of Zoe's apartment, carrying a bag of concealed cash. My revolver is in my jacket pocket in case anyone tries to take the cash, and I sincerely hope I don't have any nonsense like that, as I'm in enough of a bother as it is. I am nervous, so I try to break this feeling of drudgery by glancing out the large window at the far end of the corridor. People are going about their business like nothing is wrong, but there is something wrong. I draw my eye to a large star or, more accurately, a spider-shaped structure in the distant sky. Nobody else appears to notice it—only me. I move closer to the window, catching a better angle of it. The people below are completely oblivious. It's making a humming sound that is quite loud—loud enough for everyone to hear it—only they are not aware of it. I feel a static charge oscillate through my nerve fibres. It is at first discomforting, then somewhat pleasant. The door to her apartment opens. I'm startled, and when I look again, the structure is no longer there. I take off my wig as I'm sweating.

"Zack, I thought I told you not to call again," Zoe yells.

I try to forget the previous moment's mirage-like experience and look her in the eyes. "I want to do my share, contribute—that's all."

She gestures to me to come inside with a look that says I'm a nuisance bothering her, but I go inside.

"What's with the get-up?" she asks, referring to my wig.

"I have to keep a low profile for a while."

"I knew it! That you're up to no good. Just why is it you're here?"

"I want to be a part of my child's life. I want to know my daughter."

"How do you know it's a girl?"

Those dreams are right. She is having a girl. It must be a coincidence that I spoke without thinking, because of dreaming of a daughter I callously hand over to that strange Chief. He must have practised some kind of black magic on me, or none of this would be as weird as what I'm experiencing.

She smiles. I race over to her, embrace her, and we kiss. It feels weird, like it does not focus my mind on the moment. That night I dream of a place where there are reptilian-like creatures who are grey-green, with average-sized heads, two large oval-shaped eyes, and medium-sized mouths. They also have wings. They are like creatures you would see in '50s B-movies. They open their mouths, breathing a vapour that surrounds them. I figure it must be to get nutrients to sustain them. This thing I'm experiencing is scary and unsettling. It puts shivers down my spine and gives me nausea.

Two human males and three human females are being escorted by human-looking guards into the chamber. At the centre of this chamber, I can see a large circular-shaped bath containing what I think is electrified water. The human-looking guards have a strange luminous aura surrounding them. As they push the two men and three women into the bath, their screaming reverberates through the chamber, creating a morbid cacophony. I turn around and try desperately to wake myself up by slapping myself across the face. Curiosity motivates me to watch again as I cannot wake myself. Five of the avian/reptilian alien creatures move over to an adjacent alcove. They're each separated by a thin sheet of translucent glass. The first one disappears as light dissolves it. This light fills each of the other sections of the alcove, dissolving the aliens. I can hear a deafening noise. I'm not sure if it is the combined screams of the humans and aliens as one or the energy forming over the bath. The mouths open, chanting that turns into unsettling, if not harmonious, singing. I'm scared as this seems so real. I'm immediately reminded of seeing horror movies about the supernatural, but they never rang true with me. But this does. That aliens are possibly real scares me even more.

One of the human females levitates up from the electrified water. She opens her mouth and makes a cry like a banshee. Forked lightning-like streaks of fire hit her body, and she rises from the bath onto the floor. That aura, like the one emanating from the guards, is now visible, radiating off her. She sees me! I scream, "Help!"

I wake up screaming and shaking and hit the bottle. "That fucking Chief! He gave me these dreams!" I yell.

A few months later, I purposefully stayed away from Zoe for her own safety. She is now due in a month, and I don't have the last instalment for McKenzie. All my money went on her and the baby on the way. Eight months later, Zoe has given birth to a baby girl, Emma, as she called her in one of my past dreams months ago. It's our wedding day, and the ceremony has just finished. We're heading out of the chapel. I know—a chapel, considering what I did for a living previously. But now I have turned over a new leaf and put all that nonsense behind me. I only ever took out the bad guys, except for that poor girl, but that was the crooked cop's fault. I justify it all the time: human trash needs tidying up like all trash, and someone's got to do it—so why not me? I won't go into the bullshit about how governments take out bad people all the time because you know they do, and it had to be done or they would wreak havoc on the good people.

Inside the limo, we opened a bottle of Champagne and toasted to our new future. Zoe's mother took baby Emma for a couple of weeks while we went away. The driver seemed familiar—a peculiar familiarity that I couldn't quite place. He changed route, and when I asked him why, he replied, "There are major roadworks the other way."

I thought nothing of it as they enthused me with such happiness. Then, as the journey became more familiar, I knew where he was taking us. He pulled up outside an abandoned warehouse, took out a gun, and instructed us to go inside. I knew who was waiting for me inside: the Agent, of course. He greeted us with smiles.

The driver tied me and my new wife to chairs. He also gagged her. The Agent stared me in the eye. I knew what was coming. "Please, we go back a long way. Just let my wife go. She has recently given birth."

"Unlike you, Jauntly, I don't keep loose ends. Vengeance is an exact science that yields the finest rewards. Oh, and I will find this rewarding. You screwed up royally, and now I must clean your mess up like I always had to do in some shape or fashion."

"What are you talking about? I always carried out my assignments proficiently and on time. I got the job done."

"You cost me! You fucked up so much with the hit on the cop that it brought heat on me. I don't care about you taking out that inept idiot McKenzie. In fact, you probably saved me the trouble of doing it myself."

He takes out a knife, and by the look of his facial expression, he is going to use it. The driver is still pointing the gun at me. The Agent moves closer and is about to cut me when a cloud of blue smoke fills the room. I realise that it is the same bluish colour as the smoke when the Chief threw the blue powder into the campfire. As it billows across the room, the Chief comes out, followed by the snake creature. Zoe passes out. The snake creature slithers over to the Agent, opens his mouth wide, protrudes his sharp, slender tongue, and wraps it around the Agent's head, throwing him across the room and slapping him against the walls. He's dead. The Chief gestures with his right hand to stay back. I obey him. The snake creature turns its head completely around and releases a vapour—some kind of deathly energy—and it dissolves the driver. I turn to Zoe; she is still passed out. The creature comes closer. The Chief yells to it, "Down, Pushkeen! The damn fool has earth feline DNA somewhere in his ancestry, I believe."

He makes gestures with both of his hands, and it disappears. Here is my chance for answers, I realise. I move closer to the Chief. He grimaces, "Not before time," and vanishes. *Fuck!* is my immediate thought, but I soon come to my senses and hurry over to my wife. I try to revive her, and she's coming around. I say, "We have to get out of here now, darling."

I help her to the driver's car, and we head home. A few of Zoe's friends have a wedding party organised, and we play the role of newlyweds enjoying our special day, explaining to our guests that we would have to go on our honeymoon the following day as the plane had trouble. It was a blatant lie, but how could I explain that a snake-like creature almost ate us? I come clean. "I haven't always led a straight life. I used to be a hitman. 'Used to be' are the operative words. Something strange happened to me not so long ago, and I've changed—a fresh start—I'm through with that life. And now we have nothing to worry about. The Agent, my former boss, is dead, and I'm now free."

"How do I know for sure that there won't be any more skeletons from your closet coming back to haunt us?"

"I know because I have eliminated them all."

She grabs my hand. "Promise me you will keep us safe?"

"I promise."

Seventeen years passed, and one boring day at work as a security guard, I toiled at my duties—never anything out of the ordinary, just the boring routine of patrolling the entrance of who does and doesn't go into the local hospital. Zoe was much frailer now, and Emma was a rebellious teenager. I was about to light up a cigarette when my butterfingers dropped it onto the pavement. As I was about to pick it up, an ambulance screamed past. It gave me the most head-pounding tension I could ever get from those loud sirens.

The ambulance stopped, and the paramedics wheeled out the poor unfortunate victim. I could not see who it was, but as the paramedics wheeled the trolley closer, I dropped my cigarettes. It was

Zoe. She was badly injured. I kicked myself to awaken myself and immediately rushed over to explain who I am. I followed them through the entrance. The paramedic told me she was in a car crash.

"I need to speak to her!" I demanded of the doctor as she instructed the nurses to take Zoe to ICU.

"This man is her husband. He works at this hospital as a security guard," the nurse told the doctor.

"Just for a few moments, then," the doctor replied.

I turned to my wife. She was all cut and bruised. I tried to speak but could not utter the words I wanted to say. She spoke instead, "Zack, don't let them take her. It's now the time to find the Chief."

The doctor quickly checked her vitals and determined death. I recoiled into myself. Not only had I lost my beloved wife, but in the instant she passed away, she revealed an earth-shattering revelation— or what I came to secretly believe in the dark recesses of my mind, a prophecy. I took a deep breath, knowing that I must now find the Chief. My first instincts were to go home and take Emma out of high school. Assuming that old bastard was still alive, I knew I had to get him to listen to me. The next morning, I set out to the forest where I first encountered him.

I searched around the vicinity of the fire in the same forest where I first encountered him all those years ago. I had been here about two hours now and still no sign of him. Then, suddenly, as the moonlight was shining, I saw something in the dirt sparkling. I rushed over to dig it up. It was a vial that the Chief used before. I wiped it clean and saw it was half full of powder. Gathering up sticks and placing them into the ring of rocks, I made a fire. I took out papers from my pocket and my cigarette lighter and lit the fire. As it kindled, I added more sticks until there was enough of a fire burning. Then I took out the vial, pulled the cork off it, and poured the blue powder into the flames. There was a whoosh like all those years ago, and everything quivered as if phasing reality. I saw something coming out from the smoke. It was hard to tell what or who it was. "I thought I told you not before time!" a man yelled in a furious tone. The Chief emerged from the smoke.

"How long do you expect me to wait for answers? Hasn't it been long enough?"

"I guess you're right. I put you on this path."

"That's right. You told me when we first encountered each other that I had to follow a path, and look where it has got me."

The Chief grinned. "You think your life to date was the path I was talking about?"

"Well, yeah, sure. What else do you mean?"

"You must come to us. The blue smoke from the fire all those years ago manipulated time so you could see the future in your dreams. I also gave you the capability to see the present—my present—in the form of mirages. Come to us. There's a war going on, and that is where your correct path ends—or begins another."

The Chief walked back into the billowing cloud of smoke and puffs. I decided I had enough. After all, I had Zoe's funeral to organise.

On their way to the church, Emma is crying. I know that I'm going to have to tell her the truth—about the dream before she was born of handing her over to the Chief with no compunctions. I postpone that conversation for another day. The poor girl has gone through enough already. We arrive back at our house, and she retires to her bedroom. I can hear her sobbing. I feel so bad for her and remorseful that I gave her mother a bad life. I reach into the fridge, take out some cans, and get drunk.

I wake to a pounding headache and take a shower. As I'm reaching for the shower cream, I notice the bathroom window is open, and what I see next is something that I'm barely prepared for. I can see the long spider legs of that station in the sky, like it was all those years ago. I quickly dry myself and get dressed. I go outside and witness, visually, its full dark majesty for myself. I notice it spins, and it appears to be coming closer to me at a sped-up rate. My instincts tell me this is my chance to do what the Chief suggested—I have to go there. But how? I have no space vessel or shuttle pod, unless they decide to teleport me directly to their living room; I guess I'm fucked.

As the spider monstrosity comes closer, it looks rather smaller than I thought it would be. I notice none of the other people of this so-called beautiful world are even aware of it. It's still coming closer, managing not to crash into anything. Even crows can see it and fly away from it. My body tingles, and strange thoughts and notions invade my mind. I must be going crazy. I'm not sure if I can take much more of this because the little bastard of a thing—well, one of its legs is just right above me, and it's coming closer. Icy fear surges throughout my body, and I decide there and then: to hell with it. I back a few metres onto the street, get set, and run as I've never run before. As the station comes closer, I can see it comprises some kind of organic glass because I can see my reflection, and the glass is like it's moving or percolating. I keep running and crash straight into this organic glass. I'm covered in slime. It's difficult to move as I'm paralysed by it. Suddenly, the entire room, which is too dark to make out anything, shakes, and I can see my street disappearing through another organic window. We must be in lift-off. Then, four humans with strange auroras come into the room and lift me up. I scream, "Where are you taking me?"

They cannot respond. I struggle and scream some more, "Let me go! Just why is it you wanted me here?"

They cannot answer yet again. Instead, they throw me onto a slimy surface. I'm thinking, *That's* gratitude for you, considering they wanted me here and the fact that *they've* gone to great lengths to lure me to this... whatever you would call it. To my surprise, I'm not in any pain from the impact of being flung onto a dirty, mucky surface. Seconds later, and to my surprise, the Chief enters. He has that weird-looking snake creature with him, and thank heavens he has it tamed this time. I pull some gelatinous slime from my mouth and am about to utter the words, "What now?" to the Chief, only he turns into one of those bird-like lizard creatures and makes strange singing noises. It seems he—or his entire race—is in some kind of dark emotional and mental pain. He slowly morphs back into his human self—the Chief, that is.

I can't speak. I want to go home and be back with Zoe and Emma, but I'm in this hell. He moves closer to me and takes my hand. I still can't talk. He smiles a dead smile—a smile that exudes disappointment and also a sense of the ominous hell to come—and he speaks, "Welcome home, Zelger!"

"What did you call me? Wait, I remember—that was my name, and I was once one of you," I say, shocked and revolted by the words I've just spoken.

"You will also remember the war between us, the Targelians, and them, the Zu'urn," he says, pointing at one of those snake creatures in stasis.

"I do. I became human, but before I joined the flock containing my people—a flock of Targelians who could migrate through space to each of the two planets in our home system—something happened to me?"

"Yes. As with all of our race, we made you corporeal and then successfully transformed you into human form before wiping your memories of your Targelian heritage."

"'Corporeal?' That's right—our people are spirit-like?"

"Yes, Zelger. But only for a limited time each time."

"I am really Targelian? A bird-like reptilian alien creature like yourself who can transform into a spirit, but we can no longer do that?"

"We cannot change into spirits because the Zu'urn infected us with a disease that keeps us in our physical form."

"Those humans in my dreams—you're experimenting with them too?"

"We have to. To ensure our longevity as a species."

"Why did you do this to me? I became the worst human being that ever could be."

"Don't you remember, Zelger? It was so you could mate with a human female and produce offspring capable of switching over at will from Targelian to incorporeal form. Your daughter is our future—our survival! We are losing the war against the Zu'urn. She can give us a strategic advantage. The possibilities will be endless."

"Why can't we stay incorporeal? The Zu'urn wouldn't be able to touch us," I demand.

"You know why. Because we have lost too many of our best to make that possible for every Targelian here. We are desperate!"

My instincts are conflicting inside me. There's a battle beginning to take place in my soul—if I even have a soul. I can remember my past fully now, and there's no way I'm giving them Emma. She is the one pure and beautiful being in my two lives. They can, as humans say, "Fuck off!"

"Zelger, don't test us. You're still one of us! We need her!"

I grab the weapon of one of their guards and start firing. The alarm goes off. I had almost forgotten what a strident sound it made, even as a Targelian. I point the weapon at the Chief's head, who is still in his birdlike/lizard guise. "Listen here, Chief, or whatever you're called. Take me back and make me forget again!"

I hear slippery footsteps being made, and it takes my attention away from him. I can remember who it is. It's the Elders, our leaders. No doubt I'm going to be punished now. The leader of the Elders makes her way over. "Zelger, I told them that this experiment involving you all this time was a mistake and that no good would ever come from it. Humanity is selfish, erratic, and dangerous. I said a partly human child would never give up their grasp on their selfish, toxic reality."

"Are you gonna leave her alone?" I ask.

"We will not use the child, and I want an end to all our human experiments. Our race are not barbarians. We will die with our dignity intact," the leader of the Elders replies.

"Can you send me back to be with her?"

"I'm afraid not. You have just murdered our finest generals. You have condemned us to death. Without our generals, we have now lost the war. Extinction is upon us."

She turns around and walks away. "Wait!" I yell. "There must be some other way?"

"The Zu'urn will be here soon. This, our last outpost, will be destroyed. But don't worry—your precious humans won't even be aware, their 'Zoo Paradox' and the rest of it."

"No, I need to be with my daughter!"

"You killed us all, Zelger. Congratulations for allowing weak human emotional bonding to condemn an entire species," the Elder cries.

I hear the Zu'urn coming. Their slithering tongues always unsettled me. They break down the organic walls and sink their fangs into our bodies, pulling us until we hit their sharp fins. I think of Emma and Zoe. That's the only memory I want to die having. Our time together, despite the chaos and uncertainty, and the combined memories of two lifetimes, is the most rewarding and fulfilling. I have the guilt complex that I experienced this love, and if it causes the extinction of an entire species, then so be it. However, I am safe in the knowledge that if the Zu'urn ever try their chances with humanity, mankind will withstand them. Because if there's one thing I've learned now, it's that human frailties and all of their dark points make them stronger, and this is quite admirable in them as a species. Unlike the Targelians—they were easy prey. I'm glad I had some of those qualities while in human form, as it made me strong. Farewell, everyone and everything.

BEYOND THE STARS LIES OURSELVES

CHAPTER ONE

Lieutenant Rick Caulker experiences a fleeting thought on whether his first assignment aboard the newly commissioned spacecraft called the Searcher will become eventful or one long mundane trip. The voyage seems to have been dull so far, now that the crew is in orbit of the deep-space colony known as Zetoria. Caulker is one of three space personnel investigating a crashed alien vessel on the human colony some years earlier.

Captain Tom Weller smiles affectionately over at his wife as they watch the adjacent placid nebula on the viewscreen of the ship's bridge. Caulker simpers a smile of satisfaction, as he was the catalyst who instigated the happy couple's meeting three years earlier. It was at university where he found himself with a scientific problem. He was trying to disprove some of the well-established theories of quantum physics, such as those dealing with quantum field theory. He purported the theory concerning the "standard model," where outside forces could manipulate such a highly sophisticated alien race, especially if they had gained knowledge from far more developed minds and research on methods that humanity cannot achieve because of their physical and scientific limitations.

Caulker can jump way above these theories and interpret them with an opaque sense of vision that nobody else could see—a problem through such a rare-angle viewpoint. One afternoon, he chaired a debate, and the only participants who didn't find his findings gibberish were Tom Weller and Selena Arden, two young former students. Caulker's ideas intrigued them but quickly discovered they had become more and more intrigued with each other. Not long after, when Caulker had no accommodation because of his parents' bankruptcy, the young couple offered to put him up in their house. Since then, he views the Wellers as family.

"Beautiful, isn't it?" Doctor Selena Weller says to her husband.

"It sure is, darling. Didn't I promise I'd take you out to the most exotic, farthest reaches of space when we were on our honeymoon?"

"You keep your promises. After our honeymoon

on the Moon, I've learned that they are nice promises."

"It's our second anniversary tomorrow night. Can you think of anywhere more romantic to celebrate it? I also promise you, Selena, that your life would never be boring with me. I hope I'm living up to my pledge."

"You are keeping it so far."

He reaches out and embraces his love, and they share an affectionate kiss. This confirms to Caulker that his mentor's marriage became sealed by fate. The oval-shaped ship that is the Searcher had taken three years to arrive at Zetoria from Earth and had immediately assumed orbit of humanity's first colonial deep-space settlement. The tiny ship is the size of two jumbo jets in mass and resembles a glowing diamond set against an effulgent green nebula on one side as it assumes its orbit around Zetoria, a planet four times the mass of Earth.

"The radiation from the adjacent nebula to the Zetorian colony must have concealed planetary scans by the local scientific field studies teams," reports Caulker as he wipes the cold sweat from his brow. He has been busy studying the scans on the Zetorian surface for the last four hours. "Zetoria is also obviously a 'Super Earth' planet. Combined with its sheer size and the distance to the capital city, scans this far out would be very difficult for the local scientists."

"Can you determine how long this wreckage has been located there?" asks Weller.

"The readings estimate about twenty Earth years ago when they crashed. Should I send the findings to the surface, Captain?"

"Not so fast. We need to investigate further in case there aren't any surviving hostile aliens down there. I know this is your first assignment, Rick. You don't want to allow yourself to become overeager without first weighing the risks involved with the situation."

"It's not so much that, Captain. It's just that I never really brought myself deep down to believe in extraterrestrials, even though I used them as subjects in my theories all those years ago."

"Well, Rick, centuries ago on Earth they never believed there were planets capable of sustaining human life out there, but here we are."

"You're right, Tom—I mean, Captain Weller. Forgive me, sir; I momentarily forgot we weren't on a first-name basis like before we got assigned here."

"I'll forgive you because of your age."

"It's twenty-seven again, sir."

"Wait till you're thirty-two."

Caulker laughs with ease. Over the years, he had developed a comfortable, safe rapport with him. He watches Tom stepping over to the holo-monitor to see the wreckage for himself and witnesses him becoming enthused, like a child receiving a birthday gift. "I can see this ship comprises organic matter, with only its propulsion and interior composed of some metal alloy that is unknown to us. Were they on their way to this world or Earth?"

Caulker becomes just as exhilarated as Tom over such a notion.

"Perhaps they were on a mission to start the first contact with humanity?" asked Selena.

"It's possible, but it also could have been a malevolent intent that was their mission. We should go down there and investigate," replied her husband.

"Should we first alert Zetoria's government?" asked Caulker.

"The central government on Earth has afforded me carte blanche on how to proceed in these kinds of situations, and I think this is one of those times. So, no, Lt. Caulker. We will keep this between the three of us."

Selena turned to her husband and whispered, "Are you sure that is wise? We do not know who or what we're dealing with down there."

"You're right, but we have to do it my way. The Zetorian colonial government's relationship with

Earth's central government is under strain. It's fractious, especially over the last two decades."

"I just hope we know what we're doing."

"So do I. Prepare to land the Searcher just a couple of hundred metres away from the wreckage."

"Aye, sir," replied Lt. Caulker.

As the Searcher made its descent into Zetoria's upper atmosphere, it was subject to a little turbulence. The crew was in awe of the unpolluted atmosphere. Selena gazed out at the beautiful terrain filled with extraordinary plants and wildlife. "Look at those trees. They must be ten miles tall!" she said in awe.

"Try to find a clear patch, Lieutenant. We don't want to land the ship on a rough surface."

"I've just discovered the spot," he replied.

The ship switched into a lower-powered state to enable manual control. Lieutenant Caulker steered the Searcher with sheer skill and ease. Tom went over to him and placed his arm on Caulker's shoulder. "Nice work, Rick."

"Tom, will the Zetorian patrol detect our landing?" asked Selena.

"Highly unlikely. This ship, even though visible to the naked eye, is blind to sensors, and they have no settlements out this far. Well, what are we waiting for? Let's get out there and find out what that wreckage is!"

No sooner had Tom uttered those words than he was followed with equal eagerness and verve by his wife and Lt. Caulker. They prepared to leave the ship and step out onto an uninhabited continent of Zetoria. The ship's door opened slowly, revealing the exotic landscape outside. They quickly discovered they were near the coastline, but this was not a beach. They could hear sounds coming from alien wildlife in an adjacent massive jungle. They were now near the crash site of the alien wreck, and the smell of the decomposing organic matter that comprised its hull was repugnant to the investigating human crew members.

Tom ignored the complaints from his wife and Caulker, and his eyes were immediately drawn to the visible internal workings of the alien craft. "Some kind of propulsion system?"

Caulker walked over to look for himself. "I guess so. It looks like the power source is still active."

A deluge of ideas flooded into Tom's mind. "Captain, I'd say I can recreate this propulsion system on a smaller scale. Just think of the possibilities if we can discover how to replicate this technology."

"Tom, are you nuts?" asked his wife. "We don't know the first thing about this ship, let alone the science behind it."

"I don't know, Rick. We are still at a disadvantage here," replied Tom.

"Captain, I must implore you. If I ever had a purpose to come all the way out this far into deep space, then this is it. I can safely verify that this system uses the same principles as any transport mechanism. The laws of physics are universal. It's worth the risk."

Two days later, Caulker reassembled the alien ship's systems. He took everything out, closely studied it, and mapped out how to put them back together again. He also discovered how their system of interstellar travel worked. When they were all back on board, they reconstructed the schematics of the alien vessel on the bridge and displayed them on the monitor aboard the Searcher.

"These aliens created a synthetic inverse gravitational wave at such a small level to enable them to engage in faster-than-light travel. I believe this transported the ship out of phase at the subatomic level with normal space to their desired destination. Only something must have gone wrong because they fell out of this phased state and crash-landed here on Zetoria," Lt. Caulker explained, rather pleased with himself, to Tom and his wife, who listened with a sense of wonder.

"Nice work, Rick. It's astounding. Nothing short of amazing how they could harness something like gravitational waves on such a minuscule scale in this way," replied Captain Weller.

He then turned to his wife, and before he had the chance to say something, she interjected, "We can still detect natural gravitational waves formed after the Big Bang. I remember that when I first went to university before I switched my studies from quantum physics to medicine. This alien race must be so advanced and superior in every way. We must tread with caution."

"They may still be unaware of the crash, or it could have been a rogue ship on an unofficial mission, or they could have been the last of their kind."

"Lt. Caulker, can we integrate this propulsion system into that of the *Searcher*?"

"It's more than possible, but is it wise? Even though integrating wouldn't take long, my worry would be the effects of an inverse synthetic gravitational wave on us, Captain?"

"You let me worry about that. The sooner we get back to Earth with our findings and the greatest prize of all mankind, the better."

Later that evening, Caulker quickly and skilfully connects the alien FTL propulsion mechanism into the Searcher's engines. He finds the basic universal mechanical principles enabling him to undertake this task rather easily. The Searcher remains on Zetoria's uninhabited continent. Tom, who only has a rudimentary knowledge of quantum physics, tries to help where he can. His speciality is being a command pilot in central Earth command's space programme.

Tom witnesses the smile on Caulker's face as night falls. It is a smile of self-satisfaction at a job well done and humble self-pride. Tom allows Caulker to have his moment in the stars and walks over to congratulate him. "Nice work, Rick. You've certainly surpassed yourself yet again."

"You wanted it up and running, sir. I believe we can perform a test sequence at your leisure."

"What does this test sequence involve exactly?"

"I will recreate the gravitational wave at such a tiny scale to see if it generates, so I can get an idea of how to create one at a more increased frequency."

"How soon can you do it?"

"Any time now, I guess."

"Well, there's no time like the present. That's what they say, anyway."

"I'll begin the initiation sequence at once, sir."

"This won't make much noise, will it? Selena needs her sleep."

"It shouldn't wake her up, sir. I'll begin right away."

He methodically begins activating the initiation sequence while his captain watches in amazement at his dexterity, as if he is assembling something as simple as a seesaw.

"There, ready to go in five seconds, four, three, two, one. And go!"

They hear a whine, and light emanates from the centre of the propulsion mechanism where the gravitational wave generator is located. The whining noise grows more intense and becomes louder until it overloads, resulting in a massive energy wave radiating outward. Caulker runs to the other side of the Searcher, steering clear of the energy wave's initial impact. However, Tom is not so lucky. He withstands the impact of the energy wave, and it knocks him unconscious. Fearing the impact was fatal to his captain, Caulker quickly deactivates the generator and yells out, "Doctor Weller! It's Tom. He's—"

Selena hastily dresses herself in her robe and rushes towards the scene of her fallen husband. "Get my med-kit!" she yells to Caulker.

He obeys her request without hesitation and, luckily enough, knows where she has kept it. He offers the med-kit to her, and she grabs it, but to her and Caulker's astonishment, Tom regains consciousness and begins laughing.

"What's so funny? Damn you, Tom. You scared me!"

He gets up. "It's just, I thought I was somewhere else, someone else. I'm glad to be back."

Selena rolls her eyes. To this day, her husband never fails to pique her interest with his offbeat remarks. She turns to Caulker. "Rick, help me bring him inside to the ship's sick bay."

Caulker hurries over to Selena's location and puts his arms under Tom's, carrying him back to the Searcher. There, she performs thorough scans of her husband's physiology, right down to the cellular level. She will not take any chances, unlike earlier. "What were you thinking, Tom?" she asks as he tries to get up from the bed.

"I'm fine, apart from a few cosmetic scratches. Tell Lt. Caulker to test again."

"What, are you crazy?!" she says, alarmed. "You're both not to touch that thing until I deem it safe."

"I think you'll find that I outrank you, dear."

"I'm being serious. No more. Now get some rest."

He lays back on the bed and smiles to himself. "Sure thing, Doc."

While Tom and Selena are in sick bay, Lt. Caulker is busy assessing the readings from the ship's sensors. "That's strange and not supposed to happen." He rushes over to the main computer console. What he sees makes him shiver. "This can't be!"

Caulker checks and double-checks the anomalous readings displayed on the screen. He gets up abruptly and leaves the bridge to head for sick bay. He knows he needs to report the readings right away to his captain. As he makes his way there, thoughts of how precarious this mission is becoming race through his mind. He realises he is not accustomed to things in science going a little crazy like they are now and makes a self-discovery about how irrational he is as a man. A pointed-out fact targeted at him all his life, only he often dismissed this in disbelief. He now thinks that the other people in his life obviously know him better than he knows himself. He finds this a little disconcerting because he believed himself to be as sure as he thought he was.

He arrives at the doors of the sick bay and opens them up without a thought, only to witness the captain and his wife celebrating their wedding anniversary in the biblical sense. As the Weller couple are nearly in the midst of their violent throes of passion, something strange occurs. Tom, for a second, appears different and then is back to himself. Caulker doesn't dare point out anything because he is too shocked and embarrassed and feels voyeuristic. He speaks softly, "My deepest apologies, Captain. Doctor Weller, please forgive me."

As the naked couple put their clothes back on and, feeling more embarrassed than Caulker, who has now returned to the bridge, mortified, they giggle at one another.

"I hope he can look at us in the same way as before. We never did that before," Selena says to her husband.

"He'll be fine. I wonder what all the fuss was about to make him barge in on us. We'd better ask him."

About ten minutes pass, and the Weller couple are decent again, back in their uniforms, as they walk towards the bridge. They find Caulker is not in any way put out by the recent embarrassing encounter with their marital habits. He is much too consumed and mesmerised by the readings on screen.

CHAPTER TWO

Caulker explains the images the Wellers are desperately trying to fathom. "Captain, parts of the Zetorian buildings in the human settlement are being swapped over to somewhere else. And that somewhere else appears to be a similar settlement from a parallel reality."

Selena, piqued by what Caulker has just described, moves closer to the viewscreen. "We now know for certain that the theory of the multiverse is real. That there could be different versions of us, each living out different paths in life in subsequent alternate realities."

"My explanation would appear to confirm this, Doctor," replies Caulker.

Selena is about to take her husband's hand

when she sees how distressed he is becoming. "Tom, what's the matter?"

He doesn't reply. His body undergoes a dephasing effect, and he stumbles to the ground. "Rick, help me bring him back to sickbay!"

Caulker obeys the doctor's request yet again, and they return the captain for more medical scans. They place him on a bio-bed, and his wife wastes no time in connecting him to life support. He is now unconscious.

Selena turns to Caulker and asks, "Did you notice anything strange about the captain last night?"

Caulker becomes embarrassed at her question. The first image that comes to his mind is when he accidentally barged in and interrupted them, catching them in the act. Then he remembers something—something he had forgotten due to the shock he had experienced at that moment. "Actually, Doctor Weller, I do now remember something odd. It's embarrassing for me to say this, but when you two were being intimate last night, I saw Captain Weller dephasing as if he was having an out-of-body experience."

"What do you mean, Rick?"

"What I mean is that it appeared as if there were two of him."

"Could your theory on the matter swapping involve people as well?"

"What are you getting at, Doctor?"

Selena experiences a realisation. "That man I was with last night was not my husband! God, I cheated on Tom with his alternate!"

"Slow down here. I'm sure there's another explanation."

She reaches out to the table and grabs a small device. "I'm going to revive him!"

"Are you sure that's wise, Doctor Weller?"

"No, I'm not sure, but I need to find out the truth here."

To her surprise, she finds that she doesn't need to revive Tom Weller—whichever one he is.

"Selena, what happened to me?" he says, struggling to utter those words.

Selena nuzzles him back to his resting position. "Take it easy, darling. You must rest."

Later that evening in sickbay, Tom comes around. He feels disorientated but is getting much stronger. Selena holds his hand. "Tom, can you remember the last day?"

"It's hazy. It's like I was transported down to the Zetorian city, only it appeared dishevelled and destroyed. All I could see were ruins of the buildings. Please tell me it was a dream and that the city is still down there?"

"Yes, the Zetorian city is still down there. However, something's going on there—"

"I need to resume my command. What exactly do you mean?"

"You're not going back to the bridge just yet. I have more tests to conclude."

Selena kisses her husband on his cheek and gives him a hug. She moves over to her holo-monitor to check the results from his physical. She winces at how clean a bill of health her beloved has. "Are you sure that you're alright, Tom?"

He nods his head. When he arrives back at the bridge, he discovers Caulker staring at the viewscreen and seeming perplexed by his findings. "Caulker, what's going on down there?"

Caulker realises there and then that his captain is in a foul mood by the way he has addressed him. No Rick, and no lieutenant. So he treads cautiously. "Captain, it's not good."

"What do you mean, dammit?"

"Just look at the buildings that swapped over from the alternate reality. I mean, they are not only in ruins, but they are inverted."

Weller moves closer to the viewscreen. "You mean that reality is a mirror opposite to our universe?"

"Yes, Captain, I do. Just look at the street signs that came over from the other side. They're similar to viewing the text in a regular household mirror. You know, the text is backwards, like a reflection."

"This has gotta be a malfunction."

"No, I'm afraid not, sir."

A beeping sound resonating from the long-range sensors interrupted Caulker's concentration. This annoyed him as he was on a roll explaining the situation on the surface to his captain. It piqued his attention. "Strange."

"What?" asks Tom.

"Captain, the long-range sensors are detecting quite unusual radiation coming from somewhere about a couple of light-years away."

Tom focuses his eyes on the sensors. "There's a black hole somewhere close to Zetoria. Could this radiation be emanating from there?"

Caulker checks the readings and adjusts the sensors. "Spot on, Captain. You're right. It is a distant black hole where this kind of radiation is being emitted."

"Any significant impact on Zetoria, do you think?"

"Let's just see."

He peruses the sensor readings as if he were a surgeon examining organs in preparation for a major operation. He uses the same methodical thinking as a scientist of that calibre. "Captain, I believe it is indeed this strange radiation that's causing the Zetorian buildings to swap over from the mirror universe."

"We have to set a course for the black hole. I'll let Selena know."

Tom heads off toward the sick bay. As he walks along the corridor, he experiences strange sensations. He leans against the bulkhead and begins breathing heavily. He hears the sick bay doors opening, followed by Selena coming out. It immediately draws her to his infirm condition, and she makes her way over to him. "Tom, are you alright?"

Tom struggles to answer her. Suddenly, his body phases out of her sight, and a more sinister-looking Tom Weller replaces him.

Selena frets. She does not know what is happening to her husband. "Tom, let me get you back to sick bay."

She helps him gently lie on the bio-bed and immediately performs scans.

"You were always beautiful, my wife," he utters.

She becomes flattered and continues her scans on him. She gazes over at the computer screen to check the scan results and nearly falls back on the floor in shock at what she has seen. "You're not my husband!"

"I am the one who risked everything to save you. I guess I succeeded in the end."

"You're not my Tom Weller. You are literally a mirror image of my husband because you are from another reality!"

The mirror version of Tom becomes agitated. "Do you realise I lost everything? I looked everywhere for you! I could not allow them to find out where you were hiding. Where did you go, Selena?"

Selena reaches for a hypo-syringe and zaps him quickly, sedating him. She leaves the sick bay for the bridge. "Why are we moving, Rick?"

"Captain Weller instructed me to set a course for the black hole about two light-years away."

"What?"

"Is there something wrong, Doctor Weller?"

"I just hope that it was the right Tom Weller who gave you that order."

Caulker has no idea what she's talking about and grows more and more confused. "What should I do?"

"I guess we stay on our present course for now. And I'll fill you in while you tell me what's going on with Zetoria and everything else."

Both crew members sit down while candidly exchanging information on the problems facing them to date. Selena is incredulous, only to find Caulker is the same. "That man from the mirror universe, that 'Tom X', is now sedated in our sick bay."

"I'll erect a containment field to keep him subdued."

"That would be prudent. After that, I guess you should start the autopilot and get some sleep, Rick."

"Sure thing, Doctor Weller," replies Caulker, yawning.

"Please, Rick. Call me Selena. I'm not so fastidious about titles as the captain." Selena heads back to the sick bay to find it is still Tom X asleep on the bio bed.

Caulker comes inside and starts the containment field. "That should keep him from leaving the bio bed."

"Goodnight, Rick."

"You too, Selena."

He leaves for his quarters while Selena watches over the alternate Weller, this Tom X, who makes her very uneasy.

The next morning, Caulker is in his quarters, putting the finishing touches to something that he has been working on for half the night. He pours himself a mug of black coffee that he made a few hours earlier and, to his disgust, he can't swallow it. It is like tar. He stares at his latest contraption and takes it to the sick bay. "Doctor Weller, sorry, I mean Selena, this little thing here should bring back your Tom, Tom Prime."

"How does it work?" she asks, unsure if the gizmo is safe.

"I have mimicked the energy being used that is swapping over buildings in the Zetorian city and reversed the procedure. I mean, I can use the same principle as Tom X to bring back Tom Prime."

"Are you sure it is safe?"

"There's only one way to find out."

Selena pauses for a few moments and thinks really hard. "Do it!"

Caulker disengages the containment field and points the device's emitter at Tom X. He then powers it on. An energy field surrounds Tom X as Selena monitors his vitals. "His organs are switching over one by one within seconds." The patient jerks with movement.

"Keep him sedated. I'm almost finished."

"Okay, Rick," replies Selena.

He wakes up. Selena performs scans on him to determine which one he really is. "It's him, our Tom."

Tom Prime is weary and somnolent. "What happened to me?"

"Get some rest, dear. We will fill you in later," replies Selena.

"I think I'll call this little beauty 'The Anti-Weller Mixer'," says Caulker, referring to his new invention.

A month passes, and Tom Prime is still in his rightful reality as his wife and Caulker now address him, much to his disdain. They are much closer to the event horizon of the black hole. Selena is feeling nauseated and suspects it is morning sickness. She retreats to the sick bay and takes a pregnancy test. The result is positive. She smiles for a quick moment but then remembers, as if she is entering a nightmare, that night of passion that Caulker witnessed by accident. She wonders, *What if Tom X is the father?*

CHAPTER
THREE

The Searcher veers near the event horizon of the mysterious black hole, experiencing shaky turbulence that unsettles the crew's minds and their entire nervous systems. Selena, who is secretly keeping the news of her pregnancy to herself, arrives reluctantly on the bridge, fearing they would soon find her secret out.

The magnificence of the heavenly body astounds Tom Prime, as the black hole alludes to. He watches Caulker preparing scans and staring at its beauty and complexity with childlike wonder. He knows this is Caulker's moment, as though it took something like this to validate the young man's reasons for coming out into space. "What do you think, Rick?" he asks him.

The captain's reassertion of Caulker's ability

always instils pride in him, and he is looking forward to giving his professional opinion to him. "Words can't describe this, Captain. Performing deep interior scans of the black hole now, Captain," he replies.

Tom Prime turns to his wife. Selena is much too preoccupied with dismal thoughts of her predicament and personal quandary to notice him. He gestures to the viewscreen as if she can't see the cosmic phenomenon that features on the screen. "Are you alright, darling?" he asks.

She snaps out abruptly from her reverie and nods her head.

"You're not still worried about my alternate coming back here, are you?"

"Who's saying that he won't? There's no guarantee that Rick's invention can keep him from phasing over from the other side."

Caulker hopes that indeed his invention will deter Tom X from flipping over from the mirror universe. He watches Selena and sees how distant she is and how she is becoming distracted from her once-close friend and husband. This concerns him now. Tom X represents an unwanted, shamed family member intruding on a harmonious unit that he is now a part of. Tom X's presence is upsetting things, and he battles the deluge from the ripples caused by the unwanted visitor's distress.

Tom Prime can't answer the question his wife had brought to him. He is clueless about what outcomes there would be to this ever-dynamic situation. Caulker hears an alert. The piercing beeping from his console always breaks his concentration, especially when he becomes immersed in something. He fixes his eyes on the sensor readings and becomes incredulous at the information displayed on the tiny screen. "Captain Weller, I don't believe it. There's an alien vessel going to intercept us in a few minutes, matching the same configuration as the one that crashed on the Zetorian continent all those years ago."

Tom Prime and Selena become fearful; however, they each can't deny the exhilaration they are both feeling at the prospect of encountering "friendly" extraterrestrials.

"Isn't space getting more and more exciting by the day?" Tom Prime asks his wife and the scientist, who are both just as bewildered as he is now. "Assuming they can communicate with us, well, they may just have some answers."

Selena and the others feel shivers trickling down their spines as a humanoid shadow with white-coloured energy appears on the bridge. "Why are you trying to destroy our gods?" an eerie concert of voices asks.

Tom Prime reasserts himself. This is a step that

they trained him for: initial contact with an alien species. "I'm Captain Thomas Weller; we are from the planet Earth. We are on a peaceful mission. To whom are we speaking for the first time today?"

"You refer to us as 'aliens.' We have no name to label ourselves. We are familiar with your species and have studied you throughout your past. Turn off your scanning beams now."

Tom Prime signals to Caulker to cut the beam. "There, we have done what you have asked. Why do you think we are going to harm your gods?"

Suddenly, the humanoid figure speaks in a soft monotone voice. "Our Elders, who are also our deities, reside in the centre of what you call the black hole."

"We do not wish to ridicule your beliefs, but no one or being can survive something like a black hole."

Caulker smirks to himself, amused by the preposterous notion of their gods living there too. He is about to back up his captain, but something catches his eye. He checks and double-checks the data being displayed on the screen that came from the scans. "Captain, I think you should look at this."

The alien vanishes while Tom Prime and Selena rush over to his station. He frowns. "Those alien fools. They are sending in waves of unknown energy, hoping to expand this black hole's event horizon."

"Why would they want to do that?" asks Selena.

"To bring closer who they believe is in there," replies Tom Prime.

"Their 'gods.'"

Caulker quickly calculates the maths in his mind, which he can do since his mind works like a computer processor. "At this rate, if the expansion continues, this black hole will consume Zetoria in decades."

He takes a mental step back, ignoring the consternation showing on the Wellers' faces. He can't believe what he has just said. The moment he speaks those words, a dark realisation that he has calculated them spot-on follows, and it means millions of human lives will be lost. Similar expressions on the faces of his two mentors echo this grim inevitability.

"This can't be!" Selena says.

"If Rick is correct, and I'm pretty sure he's never wrong, then we've got to stop them," Tom Prime tells her softly.

Caulker hears him just about. The scientific consequences concern him, such as an entire planet being sucked into an endless vacuum, but also the thought of losing his future home. Caulker has the ambition of marrying a colonist someday and raising a family in Zetoria. He believes doing such a thing would not only give his life meaningful purpose but contribute to spreading all the positive attributes of human beings to the farthest stars. This is the definition of his moral compass and makeup. He is neither a religious nor a spiritual person; however, quintessential humanistic beliefs are the basis for his morality. He believes that spreading positive energy from one person to another is as scientific as weather patterns, mechanical processes, or computer computations, as it pertains to a set of fundamentals.

Tom Prime becomes certain of his next move and, without hesitation, moves the Searcher closer to the alien vessel.

Selena is curious as to what his next move entails and politely asks her husband, "What do you intend to do, Tom?"

"Well, I'm sure as hell not going to allow them to continue their quest for their gods. I can't allow Zetoria to be destroyed. I'm going to threaten them. Either they stop what they're doing or I destroy them."

Caulker agrees with his captain. He realises too that the aliens have to be shown who is in charge here. However, his mind is graced with an idea. "Captain, I think I know a way to sabotage the unknown energy beam the alien vessel is emitting without the need to destroy their ship."

Selena looks over at her husband. She knows he

is hot-headed when he wants to be, and that is something she does not admire about him at all. Caulker is aware of this too and questions privately, deep down, whether he wants to be on this mission any longer than he has to be.

Tom Prime grinds his teeth. "So, let's have it, Rick. What's your plan?"

"I think I've figured out the makeup of the beam. It's an inverse photon field that's constantly alternating on a set range of frequencies. If I try to match it, I believe I can disperse it enough to make it ineffectual."

"Try it!" yells Tom Prime.

It takes Caulker a few moments to calibrate the matrix of the dispersal beam. "I'm beginning the first emanation now."

The Searcher emits a wide dispersal beam to counteract that of the alien vessel. It rocks both ships from the ensuing turbulence, causing Selena to stumble to the floor.

"Are you alright, dear?"

She is out cold and cannot respond. Tom Prime gestures to Caulker to aid him in carrying her to sickbay. There, Tom Prime uses his gained knowledge from his wife and performs a routine bioscan on Selena. He first scans her brain, and, much to his surprise, he discovers she is only mildly concussed. "She should be fine. Just a mild concussion," he says. "Hand me that other medical scanner."

Caulker gives another scanning instrument to his captain. He takes it and nods his head in appreciation. He continues scanning Selena's entire body. When he reaches her abdominal area, the scanner registers something. Tom Prime is taken aback. "I don't believe it. My wife's pregnant. I'm continuing scans of the fetus."

"Congratulations, sir."

"I'm afraid that you're going to have to congratulate me twice. They're twins."

Caulker smiles. "That's great, Captain." As Caulker utters those pleasant words, his scanner starts beeping.

"What's that, Rick?"

Caulker, taken by surprise, checks the readings. He rechecks and double-checks. "This can't be!"

"What's the problem, Rick?"

Caulker is unable to give him a response.

"Dammit, Lieutenant!"

"Okay, just let me think about this for a couple of moments so I can actually verbalise this."

He pauses and blurts it out, "Captain, one of these babies is not yours."

Tom Prime almost swings for Caulker, but considering the history between them, he manages to refrain from doing so. "What do you mean, Rick?" he asks solemnly.

"What I mean is: you're the father of one of the children, and it appears your double is the father of the other child."

"NOOOOO!!!" yells Tom Prime.

Caulker, still reeling from the reverberations of his captain's scream, manages to recompose himself and continues scanning Selena. "Captain," urges Caulker.

"What? There's more?"

"Yes, I think you should take a seat, sir."

Tom Prime immediately understands the gravity of this strange, almost morbid situation, if it were not for the fact that two innocent children are involved. However, he finds himself becoming intent on one solution. "You have to terminate the pregnancy, Rick. She would never have to know."

"I'm pretty sure she knows."

Tom Prime didn't expect that response from his protégé and is becoming quite annoyed with him over his moral standing, which is something he has overlooked to date in the young lieutenant. "None of this would have happened if I never had that accident! Why did you insist on reassembling that damned propulsion system, Caulker?! 'Captain, I must implore you,' and all of your bullshit!"

Caulker felt those disparaging words shattering the core of his nerve fibres. The captain had never addressed him by his surname before. He now knows he's blaming him for this unique, godforsaken situation. And he realises that Tom Prime will never see him as part of his family anymore. "Captain, I'm so—"

"Just leave it! What else is it that you have to tell me?"

Caulker regains his composure and tries to shut out the hurt and worthlessness he's feeling now: one, the captain and a father figure belittling him; and two, for the captain to blame him for all that is happening. One thing he respects, though, is the chain of command, and Caulker is a professional. He clears his throat and takes a deep breath as he tries to fathom things quickly. "My guess is both children were conceived around the same time and somehow formed the one zygote. Then it split into two, thus, twins. The problem is because Tom X originates from Universe X, which is predominantly comprised of antimatter, and you from our universe, which is predominantly normal positive matter, we're going to have to transport both foetuses from Selena's womb to separate incubators; otherwise, the two will annihilate each other, killing Selena."

"Get right on it then," Tom Prime says, now becoming increasingly distressed.

Caulker accesses the medical storage compartment and, to his luck, finds three maturation incubators stored there. He realises that Selena was well prepared in advance for this long voyage. He takes two of the incubators out of storage and assembles them into the main medical systems. Next, he prepares the foetal transport system that is designed for only transporting foetuses at an early stage of development, such as Selena's, instead of the days of c-sections in the past. The maturation process allows the foetuses to develop and mature into babies using artificial means as if they were still in their mother's womb. Tom Prime chooses not to speak to Caulker as he wrestles with his inner demons of having the automatic thoughts at first to terminate his wife's pregnancy. He has feelings of guilt and fear when he must explain all this to her when she wakes up.

"I'm ready to initiate transport of both foetuses into separate pods. Shall I proceed, Captain?"

"I suppose it's now or never; by all means, proceed." Caulker observes the readings on the monitor facing him.

Tom Prime is nervous, and his voice quivers when he asks, "What if both babies get mixed up together in the same maturation incubator?"

"Then BANG! All our worries will be over then!" replies Caulker, and then smiles. "But that will not happen. Come over here and look!"

"Has it worked, Rick?"

"Oh, yes."

"I can't."

Selena coughs and interrupts this awkward moment. She is conscious. She tries to raise her head, and the two incubators instantly catch her eyes. "My baby?"

Caulker moves over to her and grins. "Two babies, two little girls."

"A daughter," replies Tom Prime.

"What do you mean, is the other baby girl dead?" asks Selena in tears.

"Explain it all to her, Rick, please! And tell everything, I mean everything!" interjects Tom Prime.

Selena gets worried. "Explain what?"

Caulker dreads the next few minutes, having to play a part that is obviously intrinsic to the role of her husband and undoubtedly Tom Prime's obligation. As he desperately tries to say the answers she needs to hear, he battles the discomfort and self-indulging audacity of having to replace him.

CHAPTER
FOUR

Two hours pass, and Tom Prime returns to sick bay. Selena moves away as he approaches her. He is not her favourite person in the world right now; in fact, his presence completely repulses her.

"Darling," he says, reaching out to her.

She turns away. She can't look at him, let alone hear his voice right now.

The com signal containing Caulker's voice interrupts this awkward moment. There is a sense of urgency in his tone, which Tom Prime can't ignore. "Captain, you're never going to believe this. The black hole is emitting gravitational waves. It's common knowledge that black holes don't emit gravitational waves. All they are supposed to do is suck matter and light into them."

"I'm on my way," replies Tom Prime as he leaves the sick bay for the bridge.

The bridge doors open, and Tom Prime enters, finding Caulker studying these gravitational waves. "Captain, the gravitational waves are not natural. They're synthetic. Someone or something has designed them with a purpose in mind and is sending them out from the centre of the black hole."

"That seems impossible. The aliens we've encountered said their gods reside in there. Could it be them?"

"You know what they say, Captain: 'There's no smoke without fire.' Maybe there's an advanced civilisation in there after all."

Caulker thinks very hard. None of this is making much sense to him. He draws on everything he knows, all that he has learned, and all the crew has experienced to date. He postulates crazy notions and surprises himself with what he discovers.

He is interrupted by Tom Prime telling him, "Lieutenant, prepare to take the Searcher into the black hole."

"Did I hear you correctly, sir? Do you wish the ship to enter the black hole?" asks a surprised Caulker.

"You heard right!"

"Aye, sir."

The Searcher makes its way through the unique

but ever-so-perplexing black hole. It comes out into a void. The crew pull themselves together as the ship makes an abrupt stop. They are taken aback by what they see next: a strange, illuminated, grapevine-like structure. Tom Prime moves closer to the viewscreen. "This must be what those aliens referred to as their gods," he says.

An unusual being appears on the bridge. It seems similar in appearance to the beings the crew encountered earlier. This being looks around, scanning the ship and crew. "You are human?" the being asks Tom Prime.

"Yes. What is this place?"

"It's for our children. We are their Elders. What you see from your viewscreen is a mechanism that works by a large organic computer system located here, and it uses the black hole to send out gravitational waves that are targeted and specific in nature, such as altering human brain chemistry. For example, when one of you makes a decision, two possible outcomes are played out in the two realities we have manipulated."

"Our universe and Universe X. That's why there are two polarised opposites of the captain," says Caulker, astonished. "Why would you do such a thing? Why are you manipulating us and our doubles?"

The being laughs a numb laugh. "Humanity glistens with negative behaviour. You radiate it, emanating evil acts from each other. We cannot allow you to infect our children with your macabre mutations—mutations that are the tainted results of our objective: to find which reality is more suitable for our children's future. To find out the correct reality where humans are intrinsically 'good'. We try to change one person's negative decision in one reality, only to discover the alternate of that person doing a similar thing again, as if the ugliness of their decisions is reflected in the alternate's decisions. Albeit with some subtle meddling from us in the said decision and resultant outcomes. It is most frustrating, as it appears humanity and its counterparts are inherently driven to mimic each other's misery by spreading their plight to one another separately in each universe, and then, with little help from ourselves, across the multiversal spectrum."

Caulker smirks, and the being gazes at him sternly. He realises that this being is aware of his disagreement. Caulker thinks for a moment. "I'm sorry, but your view of humanity is skewed and one-sided, like tunnel vision. Give us a chance and let us prove that we're not a threat to your 'children'. You are not seeing how compassionate we are as a species to each other. Did your kind ever consider the beauty and creativity—not to mention all the kindness—shown by humans to each other and their achievements and positive attributes that make up humanity? Maybe if you stopped meddling and allowed all of us and all versions of humanity to evolve by their own merits, the result may be somewhat surprising. Humans are a very self-reliant species. It has to come from within us and through our experiences in life, whether good or bad, which gives us those realisations, and that's what makes us evolve."

Tom Prime gets a little nervous. He doesn't like how precocious Caulker seems and apologises to the strange being, only to find the being becoming angrier. There is a flash, and someone else appears on the bridge. It's none other than Tom X.

"What's he doing here?" asks Tom Prime.

The strange being points at Caulker. "His so-called Anti-Weller Mixer—well, to be a little more precise, his double—gave this man you call 'Tom X' a mirror version of the device, and that has brought this man here before you."

"Caulker, you did it. Except my Caulker named it the 'Pro-Weller Mixer,'" says Tom X to himself.

The strange being moves closer to everyone and smirks pompously to himself. "You think my species is wrong? Well, let's have a little test to prove me right."

"Thanks a lot, Rick," says Tom Prime, dismayed. "What kind of test?"

Tom X becomes agitated. "Why am I back here? Where's Selena?"

"Stay away from her!" yells Tom Prime.

"Gentlemen, please. Allow me to take our host up on his test," Caulker interjects.

"NO!" A hard-sounding scream from the strange being is heard. "The test involves those two. They are fundamental opposites of each other," continues the strange being, referring to Tom Prime and Tom X as the bridge doors open and Selena rushes in.

"Why is he back here?" she asks, staring at Tom X with considerable disdain. "He's not going near the babies!"

Tom X, understandably disoriented, is taken by surprise. He takes a few moments to realise what's going on. "Did you say babies?"

Selena cannot respond. She is unsure of how to proceed in this rapidly developing volatile situation.

Tom Prime, infused with anger, charges toward Tom X. "You defiled my wife. You ruined everything!"

"What? I was sleeping alone, and then I lay beside her. I thought it was a dream. And now we have created something wonderful. Oh, Selena, how I dreamt of that short time we had that night. I'd never thought we would be together in that way ever again. I've been searching for a means to bring me back to you ever since I first found myself on this ship's bridge all that time ago." He turns over to Tom Prime. "Those babies are mine?"

"No, one of them is yours, and because you're from Universe X—the antimatter universe—you have placed my ship in jeopardy!" continues Tom Prime as he is about to swing for his counterpart. However, Tom X, being more used to hand-to-hand combat all his life, blocks him, punches Tom Prime, and levels him to the floor.

Caulker rushes over to Tom Prime and helps him get back up on his feet. He goes over to Selena and places his hand gently on her back. "How are they doing down there?"

"Oh, Rick, the babies are growing weaker by the hour. They won't survive."

Caulker moves over to the two Wellers. "Do you hear that? Both of your children are dying, and this is how you behave?"

Tom Prime reasserts himself and sighs modestly. "Maybe nature didn't intend for them to survive. This might be the only way."

Selena can't understand her husband's comment and position regarding the delicate children. She turns to Tom X. "I suppose that's your view of the children too?"

"You've gotta be kidding me?! I want those children, even my so-called alternate's child. I will fight for them; even die for them and you, Selena."

She looks back at her real husband, who is now approaching the strange being, and yells over to him, "Do you finally see, my dear husband, your alternate has all the qualities in the man that I foolishly believed were personified in you. He is the man that I thought was you."

Tom Prime has become enraged and tries to strike at the strange being. "Do you see what your meddling in science has done? You have caused my wife to turn against me, and not to mention that abomination down in sick bay!"

"Who are you calling an abomination?" yells Tom X as he charges towards his alternate. A brutal, nasty fight ensues. Selena's scream is drowned out by the growls and grunts from the two warring Wellers.

Caulker fires towards Tom X, while Selena shoots Tom Prime. Selena rushes over to Tom X. She discovers his injuries are life-threatening. Caulker checks on Tom Prime. His injuries are also life-threatening.

"Enough!" the strange being exclaims. "We have reached a determination on your species. Your people, as shown by these two specimens, are not without their surprises and puzzling considerations."

Selena drops her weapon and approaches the strange being. "Can you help my children, please?"

"Ah, yes. We can, though it will be at a cost. We must meld your children into one child, and for this to happen, we need to use strands of DNA from both Tom Prime and Tom X. Both Wellers will not survive."

Selena pauses for a moment and turns to Caulker. "What do you think, Rick?"

"I suppose you get the best and worst from both to help your new daughter to be."

Selena nods her head, gesturing to the strange being to proceed. An hour later, she has a healthy baby girl surviving in the maturation incubator. The strange being informs Caulker that the Elder aliens will inform their 'children'—the aliens who worship them—not to expand the black hole, in return for them and the rest of humanity steering clear of them for some time to come. Caulker pilots the Searcher out of the black hole on a course back to Zetoria.

CHAPTER FIVE

Ten Years Later...

A young child a few years away from her teenage years is watering hybrid plants in her back garden. She gazes up at the Zetorian sky and, like her parents, wonders what it would be like to travel through the stars and perhaps one day meet her grandparents back on Earth. She is indeed the saved daughter of Tom and Selena Weller, and her name is Anneka.

Anneka is a delightful, shy young girl. She exhibits a delicateness—a subtle frailty, like the flowers that she is watering. Her favourite is a crossed daffodil with a Zetorian buttercup-like plant that produces a pink flower and emits a sweet-smelling fragrance. She often carries out chores like this to escape the arguments her mother and her stepdad frequently have. Since her birth, the lovely romance that her mum and new stepdad had enjoyed has withered away. The arguments aren't that volatile, but more like a passive iciness between them that occasionally turns into fiery exchanges of words. This becomes a little too much for Anneka since she is aware of the principal reason they are bickering—because of her. The events from her conception to her present day. When things get heated, she retreats to the back garden and fantasises about becoming a spacefarer like her parents, which is something that she admires in both of her fathers. On her tenth birthday, Selena has told her that she is a very special girl. A child of one mother and two biological fathers. Her third parent is her stepfather, Rick Caulker.

Rick always thought it was his duty to take care of Selena and Anneka ever since the moments after they resigned their commissions aboard the Searcher. At first, his strong sense of obligation to Tom Prime instilled in him the responsibility to look after them both when they arrived back on Zetoria a decade ago. He never questions himself introspectively on this, only to become deeply emotionally and physically attracted to Selena. The fact that he had witnessed his now-wife and her first husband expressing their love months prior to the pivotal events that have resulted in his union with Selena somehow made him desire her.

Nowadays, the passion has dissipated from their marriage, and everyday problems spring up like in every union, especially where children are involved. The minutiae of marital and parental demands are taking their toll on him.

Anneka walks towards her neighbour's house, where an elderly woman named Nancy Smithers lives. She always found Nancy's house an escape from her parents, especially during torrid arguments. The Zetorian breeze blows across Anneka's face, refreshing her as she stands by Nancy's door. Something in the air inhibits the sleep hormone, thus keeping everyone perky during the daytime. Maybe that is the reason the Zetorian colonists are more efficient than their Terran cousins, and this scientific fact also contributes to the entire colony being built in years instead of decades.

Anneka wipes her brow and knocks on an old-fashioned door. Come to think about it, the whole house had been transported from Earth back in the day, brick by brick, and it was the house that Nancy grew up in as a child. The surrounding front and back gardens were also simulated to resemble the original ones. Nancy answers the door, holding a pair of cooking gloves in her hands. "Good afternoon, dear. Come in, otherwise the breeze will keep you up all night."

"Thanks, Mrs. Smithers."

"Come on, dear. How many times do I have to tell you? Call me Nancy."

Anneka smiles, following Nancy's gesture for her to enter.

She is captivated by the aroma of what the dear old lady is cooking. "Smells nice."

"It's good ole American apple pie. I'll give you a slice and some to bring home to your parents."

"Thanks so much, Mrs.—I mean Nancy."

Nancy takes out the cooked apple pie from the oven and places it on the table. "Come and look for yourself, Anneka."

She carries out the old woman's command and heads over to the table to get a better view of the baked pie. The pastry looks different. It appears to have been reversed, and the aroma of cooked apples changes into rhubarb. Nancy is momentarily taken aback, but she is indeed aware of Anneka's history and pretends there's nothing wrong at all. "Stupid woman, ain't I? I must have mixed up the apples with rhubarb last night."

Anneka doesn't think much of this. She believes Nancy's false explanation and offers to make her a cup of tea. "A cup of Zetorian weed tea, right?"

"That's correct, dear. There's some in the cupboard."

She proceeds to the location of the cupboard and opens the door. As she is about to take the tea caddy out, the picture of an alien goose facing left is now facing to the right. Anneka sighs and rubs her eyes, but the picture of the goose is still facing right. "You know, Mrs Smithers—I mean Nancy—I don't feel too good. I'd better be heading home."

Nancy stands up slowly, as she's no longer young and is often weary at this time of the day. "Please, don't go yet. I get few visitors nowadays."

Anneka empathises with Nancy to the point of even pity. "I will stay and have some tea with you, after all."

She continues preparing the tea and hears Nancy instructing her to have some baked cookies to go along with it. Anneka reluctantly opens the other cupboard and sees the label text reversing as if seen through a mirror. Nancy peers at her from a distance. However, due to her failing eyesight, she is oblivious to Anneka's plight. So Anneka takes a deep breath, puts two cups on a tray and a plate of large home-baked cookies, and slowly carries them over to the coffee table, trying desperately not to suffer more psychotic episodes that she believes she's now experiencing.

"Thanks, dear," Nancy remarks as she witnesses

the fruits of her labour, seeing the hot baked cookies. She takes one, trying not to burn her fingers as Anneka pours the tea.

"Exquisite, I think you'll find, dear," she says, taking a small bite of the cookie. "Now, it's my time to show you some sympathy, dear."

"What do you mean?"

"Come on, Anneka. I'm not so old that I don't know you're only staying with me out of pity. Please, tell me just what's on your mind, darling."

Anneka rolls her eyes in a good way and smiles. "Did you really get the apples and rhubarb mixed up last night?"

Nancy sighs. "You got me there. No, I didn't get them mixed up at all. I'm quite methodical in everything I do. Not even old age can change that."

"I figured as much. I heard the stories about the time when I was born on board the Searcher with my parents and my alternate father, who is my true father—or half my true fathers."

"It doesn't matter how you came into this world, Anneka. The fact that you're a genuine and beautiful young woman is all that counts."

Anneka is close to tears now. She can barely hold them back. "What if that chaos returns and I caused it all right back when I was born?"

Nancy isn't sure how to answer her question. She is too old and feeble for her mind to think exotic thoughts such as Quantum Mechanics. She simpers distress, which is not intended as a reply to Anneka's question to hint at her to buzz off, but because she is no longer agile. "I'm so sorry, dear. You'd better continue this conversation with your folks."

"Okay. I guess nobody can answer my questions. I'll return home. Thanks for the tea and sympathy."

As Anneka heads out the door, there is a fervently guilty streak surging through Nancy, as a little part of her is glad to be rid of Anneka.

But Anneka is much too preoccupied with her mental well-being for the taste of the old woman's cooking to stop her in her tracks.

"You seem troubled, dear?" Nancy asks Anneka.

"It's nothing."

"It certainly isn't nothing, by the looks of it."

CHAPTER SIX

Another Ten Years Later...

Anneka, now 20 years old, watches her new neighbours move into Nancy Smithers' old house. Nancy passed away a few months back, which distressed Anneka. The Stapletons had come from Zetoria's outlying towns from the capital city, and with them was their five-year-old daughter named Natasha. Over the years, Nancy secretly regretted being harsh to Anneka on the day she came around for tea. So she turned a blind eye to the various mishaps that took place in the ensuing years prior to her death, much to Anneka's comfort.

Rick comes out of their own home to find his stepdaughter. It isn't too long before he figures where she may be. He approaches her, smiling. "How are the new neighbours getting on?"

She returns the smile. "Fine, I guess. You know, I'm really gonna miss Nancy."

"I know, sweetheart. I know. Come on, it's time for supper. Your mother's even cooked apple pie that closely emulates Mrs Smithers'."

"That sounds good."

That evening, Anneka eats much of the pie until her stomach hurts. Then things go awry again, like objects swapping over from Universe Prime to Universe X and vice versa at a more exponential pace. Selena sighs and is becoming extremely concerned. She glances over at her husband, and Rick acknowledges her concern by his facial expression. She tries to speak about the elephant in the room, but Rick turns on the colony-wide holographic news service, featuring stark and chaotic images. There is a mass transference of objects from both universes taking place at once, like cars, where particle by particle and atom by atom they are transferring and swapping with their counterpart particles—atoms and molecules from Universe X—thus rendering them inoperable. Buildings are also swapping over, causing entire structures to implode with heavy loss of life. Selena can't bring herself to accept that this nightmare is happening all over again, but this time on a macro scale.

Rick hears his private com line being accessed. He excuses himself, saying it's only his work, but the fact is nobody at work even has access to his com line. He is in his private study and shuts the door. The ID code displayed on the tiny LCD screen is gibberish. He cautiously answers, "Rick Caulker."

"This is also Rick Caulker, your alternate double communicating to you from what you refer to as 'Universe X.'"

"What do you want?"

"The same thing you do. Order. That child—a Weller child—is the focal point of the displacement wave that is upsetting the intrinsic makeup of both our realities. This displacement wave is causing the transference of objects from one universe to the other. Soon it will be people, just as both Wellers were two decades ago. And now we have evidence of an imminent mass swapping of random areas throughout the space-time continuum, where at first there is a transference of objects and people from one universe to the other, and then swapping back again as if like a flip-flop effect. We have seen people permanently disfigured because of this. Their organs are half their own as well as part of their counterparts. Listen to me and end this mayhem!"

Rick Prime stops and thinks for a second. He is unsure whether he can trust his alternate, especially if he is a bad person like Tom Prime's double turned out to be. "Just how are we supposed to stop this?"

"Simple. By terminating that abomination that you call a young woman."

"We will not!"

"You must. Killing her is the guaranteed salvation of both our universes."

Rick Prime ends the call, as a conflicting dilemma runs through his head: should he listen to the evil barbarian Rick X when he knows deep down he is right regarding putting an end to this chaos spanning two parallel realities? Or should he ignore the fact that Anneka is the focal point?

Selena enters Rick's study. She immediately notices him being preoccupied with this perplexing situation. "It's Anneka, isn't it? She is the cause, right?"

"I'm afraid so. My alternate contacted me from the other side."

"You don't believe that monster, do you?"

"No matter what he is, he's telling the truth. Anneka must die for things to remain stable."

"Oh, God!"

Selena breaks down. Her husband reaches out to console her. "I'm so sorry for everything, Selena."

This moment of receiving solace from one another's plight and empathy for their daughter abruptly ends when they witness the front door slamming. Selena experiences the most shocking of realisations. "She overheard us."

"I'll go after her," replies Rick.

"No, she always preferred time alone to think. She'll be back, and we will both explain everything to her."

Rick thinks. Something is itching in his mind. He can't help but think that there has to be another option.

Anneka retreats outside of the Stapletons' old house. She misses Nancy terribly and wishes she were alive right now. Her thoughts are jumping through hula hoops in her mind, and she is consumed by fear. Fear that only could result from such distressing thoughts. That she is the sole cause of this mayhem is giving her a virulent sense of guilt. After all, she didn't ask to be born into the circumstances giving rise to her conception. It was a horrible accident that marred her existence right until now. She now knew the very stars that she once longed to explore caused all this calamity. If her parents had never come out here, then she would be normal.

She is about to cry until the solemn tear that is about to drop from her eye becomes a singular tear as she, in turn, hears the cries of young Natasha. She proceeds to their back window and sees something horrible happening to the young girl. She is morphing into two people: herself and her alternate from Universe X.

"No!" and with that exclamation, she knows what must be done. She searches for the wild leaves surrounding the house. Nancy had always told her they were poisonous. She plucks one and ingests it. The deadly bitter taste rapidly infuses her with the toxin. Anneka passes out and is no more. Natasha reverts to her normal self.

Rick and Selena switch on the holographic news. It details the return to normality. They immediately realise the unthinkable and search for Anneka. As they are about to exit their front door, they see the Stapletons carrying Selena's body to them.

"No! No! My beautiful girl," cries Selena.

Rick tries to console her, but she resists him. The thoughts plaguing their minds are: Anneka overheard them earlier and must have believed that ending her life was the only solution. These thoughts later got even grimmer as Rick discovered much too late that the augmented DNA that was first manipulated by those Elder aliens could have been altered to balance the displacement wave in their favour. Rick and Selena are inconsolable and eventually return home to Earth, each never reconciling the events since they first disembarked on their mission to Zetoria. Selena never finds it in herself to recover from the permanent guilt of knowing her precious, unique Anneka overheard that fateful conversation that cost her daughter's life.

THE AFTERGLOW

CHAPTER ONE

As Ted Malone gazed upon the horizon from outside his house on that frosty Tuesday morning, he thought how tranquil the world seemed to him in his new hometown of New Cedars, Alaska. The new east side clock face sparkled as the golden sun reflected off it. Ted thought it strange as the figures on the front were glowing – the twelve, the three, the six and the nine, not to mention the steel figure of an owl on the top of the tower's spire. He guessed it was the result of the mayor's quirky personality traits. The soon-to-be re-inaugurated four-faced clock tower that adjoined the town hall was striking in its appearance. It had been just recently reconstructed and was to have an official civic ceremony in a few days.

Ted's wife and family were still cleaning up after breakfast, and his teenage son had cycled to the local high school, where Ted was a science teacher. His daughter was always trying to outshine the other girls at the school. She wanted to be an actress, and he thought she had what it took to be one. She wasn't precocious or pretentious. She was a sensitive, empathetic girl. His son, on the other hand, just wanted to live each day at a time, enjoying what life had to offer. Then there was his youngest daughter, Adele. She was only seven years of age. She was like an angel to him. Of course, this was a biased father talking. Finally, he and his wife, Lorna, had their ups and downs, but he believed that he could always count on her, and she was still there when it mattered.

There he was, teaching a group of rowdy fifteen-year-olds when his neighbour, Bill Stravinsky, knocked on the classroom window. The kids laughed and chanted, "That's ol' Cranky Bill!"

Bill was a slight misanthrope but harmless. He was single and in his sixties. Ted figured things or life hadn't quite worked out for him in the way he hoped. Bill looked at Ted through the glass with a stern expression and signalled to him to come outside.

What does the old crank want now? Ted thought.

He was always complaining about someone or something. Ted stepped out of the school building, and Bill was waiting for him in the car park.

"Tensions between the Russians and us are at breaking point. There's not long now. Small wonder when you just look at how this world is going," Bill said.

"Bill, I have a class to teach! I don't need news updates from you. I'm sure this nonsense will blow over," Ted instilled in him, or at least he tried to instil in him. Bill just frowned and walked off home. Ted went back into the classroom. The uneasiness worsened, and he couldn't help but think – Was Bill right? Even though he sounded delighted by the prospect of the world ending. Political tensions were dangerous throughout the world at this time. The students were busy doing everything but learning, and he remembered yelling at them harshly to get back to what they were doing before the interruption from Bill, but he couldn't help but think Bill was right. Populism was on the rise, and Russia was gaining territory in Eastern Europe. Tensions were very high, and it was only a matter of time before something happened. Ted now just wanted to spend the entire evening with his wife and family.

On this day was the official reopening of the town hall. Mayor James Kelly was giving a speech when Ted finally arrived there. As Mayor Kelly concluded the statement, Ted gazed over at the crowd, then looked away and witnessed Bill Stravinsky spitting on the ground. Ted became revulsed at Bill's behaviour and thought it very hateful. *What could he have possibly against the mayor?* he thought.

On his way to the car, Ted heard a weird sound – kind of how Ted imagined electricity would sound as it flowed, if there was such a sound – followed by a bright, unblinding flash that felt almost comforting. He was dazed for a moment and straightened himself up and looked around him. The rest of the people nearby were experiencing the same. Some broke into tears at the realisation that it was an attack, the beginning of World War Three. Ted quickly checked his skin, and he became consumed by an icy fear that he was going to break out in lesions. He got into his car, and to his surprise, it started. He quickly switched on the radio; there was only static. His mobile phone was down, too, as he discovered when he tried to call his wife and kids. He drove home.

When he arrived back home, Lorna was seated on one of the armchairs in the living room, holding Adele, who was crying. He rushed over to them and held them tight.

"Where's Bridget and Christopher?" he asked his wife.

She shook her head.

"So it has begun, hasn't it?" she replied.

"I'm afraid so. I better go back out and find the rest of our family. We're better off all together."

"There's not long now. How can you protect us from the inevitable?"

"At least... we will go together as a family."

Tears fell from her eyes as she cuddled Adele. "We will have an evening supper soon. I suppose the vegetables I grew out in the back garden are all contaminated. It won't make a difference because we're all going to get sick soon."

She said the word "sick" lowly so Adele wouldn't hear it.

That ominous thought was interrupted by the sound of the phone ringing. Lorna was nearer to the handset, so she answered it.

"Ted, it's for you. It is Mayor Kelly."

He quickly moved to the opposite side of the living room.

"Hello, Mayor Kelly."

"Ted, it appears established communications to the outside world were severed, as with the rest of the state of Alaska. We have to band together to establish contingencies for what we're going to do next. I'm holding a special city council tomorrow at two pm. May God have mercy on us all."

"Count me in, Sir."

He then hung up. He figured he had a long list to

inform. He was surprised that the local underground landline was still operational. That was a plus. Lorna called him over for supper. He helped her serve it. Her hands were trembling as she handed out the food. It was pasta. He looked out the window and noticed the ribbon was sparkling, and it then began to emit short bursts of light that lasted for a few moments. He started thinking this was indeed an extraordinary phenomenon that could be starting another stage in whatever experiment it was intended to be.

Later that night, he waited up for Christopher. Bridget was on the other side of town, devastated and fearful of more attacks. She decided to stay at her best friend's house. Ted was sleeping in the armchair when he heard the key turning in the keyhole. He opened his eyes. He was somnolent, but he could make out it was Christopher coming inside. He appeared to be distressed.

"Son, are you okay?"

"Sure I am, Dad. Those bastards in Washington and Moscow decided to ruin it all for the rest of us. What a bunch of assholes."

"I know, son. So sorry your life is irrevocably changed."

"Yeah, for everyone."

"Can I ask you how Jennifer is holding out?"

Jennifer Fernandez was Christopher's girlfriend.

She was the same age as him and very pretty. Her family moved up here a year and a half ago from southern California.

"I've something to tell you, Dad. I suppose it doesn't matter now anyway, even if you and Mum get mad."

"What is it, son? Spit it out."

"Three weeks ago, Jennifer found out that she was five weeks pregnant."

"What?"

"Please, Dad, let me finish."

"Sorry, go on."

"Earlier today, we were at Doctor Smithers's practice, and it was when the attack and bright flash happened. He immediately went over to Jennifer to check her and the baby, but what he found rattled him... rattled all of us. She was not pregnant."

"Son, I don't know what to say."

"There is more, and her scans showed no evidence that she was ever pregnant in the first place."

"What? Doctor Smithers became incapable – he must have missed it, or his equipment malfunctioned due to the flash."

"No, Dad. Neither. It was not a miscarriage. It was as if someone erased our baby from history."

Ted didn't know how to respond to what his son had just said. He hugged him, and Christopher went back to Jennifer.

The next day, Ted was at the town hall with Lorna. Mayor Kelly was there early, as was the city council. They were discussing emergency backup plans for situations like this. This town meeting was called by Mayor Kelly, and joining him were Father O'Reilly, Pastor Thompson, as well as members of minority faiths. As they made their way there, the luminous ribbon was pulsating that afternoon. Lorna turned to her husband and said, "This couldn't be nuclear. Just look at those waves of light up there. It's more profound than we think."

"Or it could be caused by a new weapon of some kind – one we've never heard of before," replied Ted.

They arrived at the town hall to a packed street filled with every age of the town's population. Ted felt ashamed that he didn't bring the kids along. There were emotions of fear, uncertainty, and some apathy from everyone. They got out of the car and headed inside. There was muttering about what had happened and what was to come. Mayor Kelly entered the chamber, and there was a quick silence.

He cleared his throat. "My fellow citizens," he said. "As we are all aware, New Cedars seems cut off from the outside world, and we are at a loss as to what is going on out there—"

He was interrupted when Ben Zimmerman barged in and yelled, "I just came back from Wilson.

Skeletons were lying on the streets. The buildings appeared as if they weren't attended to in decades."

Mayor Kelly urged restraint. Nobody could understand what he was saying, but Ted knew. Whatever happened to the town of New Cedars, it was now in the distant future. He decided to keep that realisation to himself. There was enough uproar as it was without him adding to it. Ted walked out quietly, and Lorna followed him. They headed for the car and drove home. There was silence throughout the journey. Ted was thinking to himself, *Just what in the hell is going on here?*

When they arrived back home, they heard Adele crying. He quickly went to the back garden to find she had fallen off the swing. What he saw next blew him away. Her leg was severed, and in its place on her body was a limb composed of energy and light. Lorna was coming around the back with the first aid kit, and he yelled at her to get back. Adele saw how revulsed her father was, and it must have made her feel even more scared and alone. He reached out and held her.

"We have to take her to the hospital. It could be some kind of radiation poisoning," said Lorna.

"Agreed," Ted replied, and then he turned to his daughter. "Don't worry, sweetheart. Everything will be just fine. Daddy's here now."

In saying that, he knew he was not her father,

but he just couldn't bear to see her upset. He looked to find Lorna was in a state of shock. She dropped the first aid kit from her hands. He simpered to her that he had everything under control. She was speechless. They carried the child inside and laid her on the sofa. Lorna went inside to the kitchen to get her a glass of juice. She sobbed on the way. He couldn't stop the deluge of questions firing in his mind. First, there was the Flash that didn't kill any of them, then there was the town of Wilson which seemed to have aged decades, or it was destroyed long ago, but he was there himself only last week, not to mention his son's non-existent baby and now this. He had no answers.

As they both lifted their daughter into the car, their neighbour, Mrs Clarke, spotted Adele and the limb that was beaming energy where her lower leg should be. She screamed and went back to her house. Adele was staring at the limb. She cried out, "I want to be a little girl again!"

He turned to Lorna, "Change of plan. Take your car and bring Adele to the cabin. You both will be safe there until I know what to do next."

"Okay," Lorna said, sobbing as they both brought Adele to the car.

As he saw them drive off, tears fell from his eyes, and he headed back inside. His grief was interrupted by a knock on the door. He got up to answer it to tell whoever was there to go to hell, and to his surprise, it was Bill. He was smiling.

"Ted, I have someone here who has all the answers to your questions."

A strange, svelte man came into view. He was expressionless, and Ted had never laid eyes on him before.

CHAPTER
TWO

Bill Stravinsky left Ted Malone at the school and thought to himself, *What a jumped-up little know-it-all.* Bill continued home. He'd lived by himself for over thirty years now, and loneliness was something that he had surpassed in becoming accustomed to. In one way, he wished this damned, Godforsaken world would end and allow things to reset; only it would be all the same soon enough again. Being what people are, he figured it would never get any better.

He reached into his pockets and took out a packet of cigars, only to discover, to his great annoyance, that he was out. *Don't tell me that I have to go back down to that fucking store to buy some more.* Not to mention it was Malone's eldest daughter who was working there at the moment. He didn't like the way she looked at him with such disdain, as though he were something not belonging in her pretty, neat little world. As if he had to be exterminated to purify her small world of so-called ordinary people who only had the right to live in it, he believed. He knew he sounded paranoid, but hey, he thought, that's him all over. He always described the word paranoid privately to himself, like saying *pre-annoyed*. He would become annoyed, very annoyed, about a future dire situation that he knew would probably happen, and the bitch about paranoia was that it seemed to be contagious. He believed he made other people paranoid about him in turn because he came to realise that when he was surrounded by that grey, hazy cloud, he drew a lot of attention to himself, and when they saw him again, they automatically assumed the worst – that he, at present or presently, would be paranoid. He believed he couldn't win.

Bill had suffered from mild paranoia since he was in his early twenties due to a chemical imbalance in his brain. It caused him to be left on the fringe of society and led him to be self-destructive. As he walked by the civic ceremony to reopen the clock tower and heard Mayor Kelly concluding his speech, he spat on the ground out of disgust. Bill always believed it was his idea to have reflective numerals of twelve, three, six, and nine, and also to have a steel ornament of an owl on the clock tower's spire. He told everyone in New Cedars who would listen for a moment or two—before they walked away—that it was all his idea, his design, which Mayor Kelly had stolen from him over eighteen months ago. Bill had the crazy notion that the mayor had his house bugged. The owl was his mother's favourite creature, whom he'd lost at a young age, while the numerals set at fifteen minutes were what he believed was the duration of time required by him each hour to have peace from his overworking mind.

Bill made his way back to the store to purchase more cigars when his eyes were drawn to a bright, unblinding, effulgent light on the southern horizon. People fell to the ground.

That was it. It was a nuke. They finally did it! he thought. He opened his eyes and quickly checked to see if he was still in one piece. He was, so he got up and gazed at where the light had originated in the sky. There was a bright yellow ribbon of light across the sky.

There was no mushroom cloud, just a beautiful-looking streak of golden light in the sky. It must be some kind of advanced nuke/bio-weapon hybrid, he thought to himself, as the rest of the townsfolk got up too and began staring at the streak of light in the sky.

His counsellor wasn't going to believe him when he told him about the light in the sky. His approach was to break down his delusions and try to rationalise them right down to ground level. "What do I tell him now? That I have developed full-blown schizophrenia? It seemed that I was getting worse, or the Russian bomb had missed the town of New Cedars, Alaska, and the hazardous biological fallout would eventually eradicate us all."

He figured how he would like to see his counsellor's talk-therapy attempt to solve this quandary of his. It was a battlefield in his head with the paranoid fantasies versus the forces of the rational, in the form of counteracting positive thoughts against the subject he was deluding on. As much as he tried to avoid people, he would be lonely if he was suddenly all alone on this fair planet of ours. He thought, *What good is having a personality—even a lousy one like my own—if you can't interact with your fellow man, even if that's a mostly negative interaction, to begin with? If nothing else, a good argument when I'm feeling abrasive is interaction in itself, like a good debate on current affairs. What I'm trying to make sense of is interaction, even if it's negative. No one wants to be alone. If death was to occur to me soon or befall us all, then what next?*

Maybe death is the finality of one's earthly existence, or possibly their essence or soul moves onto a higher plane... maybe even Heaven. He never entirely made up his mind on that one, and it was the much unknown outcome of this pivotal question that kept him going all these years. He believed we were all going to find out for ourselves soon enough. All he wanted, all he craved, was peace at the end of his sorry life.

He arrived home. It was his family's house for two generations. He was a loner, maybe because he was an only child. He opened the back door because he didn't like his neighbours watching him go inside. He found them intrusive and invasive, especially the way he thought they looked at him. When he got inside, he noticed his things were not in their usual places. Someone was in here. He felt like killing whoever it was. He yelled, "Who's here?"

A tall, thin, weird-looking man came over to him. Bill didn't see where he had just come out of. He wasn't smiling or mad at him, and he didn't feel threatened by the stranger. "Who are you?" Bill asked.

The stranger spoke to Bill, and the words sounded like they were sung, not said.

"I am here to tell you that our experiment has failed and must be reset. You are an individual, one of many, who can help us to reset our experiment so we can re-initialise it."

What was he talking or singing so strangely about? Bill asked himself. Maybe it was his condition finally deteriorating even more, he thought.

"Look, pal. I don't know what your game is, but I need to take my medication now, so please get out of my way."

"You don't require medication."

"Now I know I'm hallucinating," he said, pushing him out of the way as he headed over to the cabinet to get his pills. He opened the jar and swallowed two of them without taking a glass of water to wash them down. He was out cold for a couple of hours. When he awoke, he found the weird tall man still staring over him, and again he startled him with his presence. "Just say that you're not a figment of my imagination and that you are really here. Just what can I do for you?"

"We require two of the individuals to undo this experiment."

"You probably mean you want me to offer myself up to die?"

"Yes. You are one of us. The person you think you are is already dead."

"What do you mean?"

"The individuals who currently reside in New Cedars believe they are themselves, not one of us, and have already died."

Bill decided to give him the benefit of the doubt, or else it was a new delusion he was now experiencing, so he went along with it just to see how it would play out.

"You said that you need two of us?"

"Yes."

"Well, I just happen to know someone else who would be more than happy to help. His name is Ted Malone."

"Please take me to him at once."

"Sure, I will."

Bill was thinking to himself that if this shit wasn't in his head, Ted Malone was much smarter than him, and he would figure out what was going on here. Bill gestured to the stranger to follow him out the back door, and as they were now heading to Ted's house, which was just a few blocks away, Bill couldn't help but notice that damned light in the sky.

"Do you see it too – the light in the sky?"

"Yes, I do. It is called the Afterglow."

"It has something to do with all of this, hasn't it?"

"Yes, it has."

CHAPTER THREE

"Bill, what do you mean he has got the answers? Just who is he?" Ted asked Bill.

"Please, Ted. Let us in."

Ted decided to disobey his instincts because he was indeed desperate to find some explanation for everything that had been going on. "You can begin by telling me what that sparkling light in the sky is."

The strange man stepped inside and spoke.

"It is what we call the Afterglow, and it is a result of the process used to copy all memory engrams of the citizens of New Cedars before the Flash occurred, and then, in turn, these engrams were transferred to alien hosts. We needed to do this because the original inhabitants were all killed by your last World War."

"But we are alive!" Ted yelled at him.

"No, Ted Malone is dead, killed by nuclear war. You are a copy of him. You are one of us," the strange man continued, and then he turned to Bill. "So are you. You are, in essence, energy beings who have been morphed into humans by these recorded engrams. You have forgotten your alien past."

Ted laughed out loud.

"Get out! You're as bad as Bill here. Now I know that this is some kind of ruse because you're expecting me to save the world with someone like him. The man's a raving lunatic. Everyone avoids you, Bill, for a reason, because you portray all that's negative in the world," Ted said insensitively.

"You think that you're something, Malone, don't you? It's alright for you growing up in perfect New York City with your perfect little life, wife and kids, and your social standing. The rest of us have to make do with little, God-forsaken shitholes like New Cedars. You're just like everyone else in this town – thinking I'm compromised – I'm still a person behind this affliction! Sorry if I'm not as perfect as the rest of you in regard to fitting into your perfect little town or what your limited intelligence perceives as 'normal', but hey, thanks for confirming my longest paranoid suspicion of what the entire town thinks of me!" Bill replied, bitterly angry.

"How fucking dare you?! You believe that you are the only one who has it bad?" yelled Ted, then paused for a moment to think. "I get the impression, Bill, that you would be the same no matter where you came from or no matter what changes in life you would blow. You see, we all have obstacles in life, each with their problems. I'm just one of those people that are better able to overcome and handle them. Granted, I don't have a condition like yours, but for the record, New Cedars is a paradise compared to NYC. The sooner you stop allowing your 'affliction', as you call it, to blanket-hate everything, the better off you will be."

"I may blanket-hate, but at least I don't engage in selective bigotry, and I really don't care, come to think of it, if the entire human race is wiped out. They were nothing but self-centred bastards anyway."

"Did you ever consider why some people may avoid you? It's because sometimes you seem very angry, like you're enveloped in a conflux of self-rage. You should try to lighten up because, Bill, life's much too short."

Ted knew he was right and felt a little ashamed of his stereotypical preconceived conception of Bill he had – not just then but over the years too. Something deep inside hinted to him that he would have to accept Bill as an equal and place his frailties aside if they were going to have any chance of defeating the aliens.

Ted was still experiencing some denial but knew deep down that this being was right.

"Why was all of this done?" Ted asked the strange being.

"The purpose of our experiment was to see what made human beings tick. This was the first phase. Phase Two will involve unpleasantness, such as physical and mental torture."

"None of us are human? We're like you?" asked Bill.

"That's right, Bill. We are beings composed of pure energy. When the process *'copied'* the memories, thoughts, and sensibilities of your human counterparts into you – you became them wholly. You are more than mere copies, and you are, in essence, Bill Stravinsky and Ted Malone just as much as their biological selves were."

Bill was saddened by what the being had just said and struck him.

"You had to give the paranoid one's memories to me. Why?"

The strange being didn't respond.

"Well, I'm glad Bill Stravinsky is dead. His life was meaningless and full of mental torture. I hope he rests in peace like his idea for the clock tower," said Bill, somewhat relieved.

Ted circled the floor and blurted out, "Why come clean now? Why didn't you just leave the experiment running? God knows we'd all be better off."

"Because the experiment was immoral to a few of us, like me. We fundamentally believe it is wrong, and it has to be played out until virtually the final instant," the stranger said, turning to Bill. "You are still as much Bill Stravinsky, even if you don't care to be. You will continue to have his psychological ailment until all of this concludes. I suggest you both work together and prevent intolerable suffering."

Bill laughed. "Let me tell you something about *'intolerable* suffering.' That is walking down the street where everyone is either avoiding you or looking at you funny or both. Sooner or later, it all adds up and makes you question your place in the world."

Ted remembered something as Bill was venting. "You know, Bill, people haven't always treated me fairly either. I didn't have it as easy as you believe. Growing up, my father passed away when I was young, and I remember being in high school, completely useless when it came to football. I was always a nerd. That's why I became a science teacher—"

"Is there a point to this, Malone?" Bill asked, mildly interested.

"Yes, Bill. There is. When I was alone, I thought really hard and decided to forgive the other students at school for mocking me and excluding me. In doing that, I gained a sense of peace that gave me the momentum to move along. I've since applied this philosophy numerous times, and guess what? It always gets me on my way."

Bill smirked but then made an expression as if he were intrigued by what Ted had just told him.

"The Afterglow? Can we reverse it?" Ted asked the stranger.

"Yes. We can't get rid of it, so we are forced to reset the experiment over."

"This is where it gets really interesting, Malone. They need two of us to prevent Phase Two."

"Is this true?"

"Yes."

"Well, count me out! I have a family to mind!"

"Either way, your family will not exist again. If you are unsuccessful, my race will choose another time to travel back, and they will understand human behaviour absolutely so they can invade, conquer, and enslave."

"You can travel in time?" Bill asked.

"Yes."

Ted was showing signs of thinking very hard about what was going on. "You caused World War Three, didn't you?"

Bill became repulsed by the strange being's neutral facial expression.

"It was necessary to speed up their timetable."

"Ted, we can't let them go back and destroy the human race in the past!" Bill cried out.

"Okay. What do you need us to do?" asked Ted to the strange being.

"I already told you that my people can manipulate time. I need you to hijack the Afterglow, return to your human bodies, and destroy the lens. The lens is the mechanism used to create the Afterglow in the first place. Without it, none of this will ever happen."

Bill was in disbelief. He shook his head and began grunting to himself. Ted saw how Bill was behaving and turned to him.

"I hope you're not going through one of your episodes again, Bill?"

Bill became angry. "No, I'm not having an episode. Why do people always think I'm out of it? I don't believe time travel is possible. Maybe *you* are right, Ted, and this is a government experiment?"

The strange man began to change. His skin became discoloured, and within seconds he transformed into a being of shining bluish light and energy. Bill touched the being in his natural energy state. He quickly transformed back into a more humanoid form.

"The way you saw me moments ago is my true appearance. Trust in me. Your government is nowhere near advanced enough to create an illusion like that. One more thing—please don't ever touch me like that when I am in my natural state."

"Trust him, Bill. We need to go back and stop the enslavement of the human race and return to our bodies. Will you help me?" asked Ted.

"It doesn't make sense, that's all. Call me a backward, paranoid human being, but I—"

"—need to know how?" asked the strange being. "I will tell you. Look up at the Afterglow. It is how the aliens intend to use the memory engrams of the New Cedars population, recorded in the ribbon. These memories or engrams share everyday events anchored on any specific time in the past. The aliens' collective consciousness can find these anchors and push their collective essence to that location in the past. The intermittent bursts of light you both probably have seen enable their memories to travel back through time to themselves to communicate the results of the experiment. You two must use this means, travel back through the bursts, and destroy the lens."

Bill rolled his eyes and uttered to himself, "Sounds like what I try to make of my medical diagnosis."

"I thought those *'bursts'* were part of a weapon. It is all incredibly fascinating—using light waves in the present to transmit memory engrams back into the consciousness of an individual in the past. If this plan works and we succeed, I will be able to write a very notable paper on this theory," Ted said. "Just how do we achieve this?"

The stranger replied, "Find the location of the lens in the present. Nearby it are pods that will enable your consciousness to travel back in the next burst of light."

"Count me out," Bill said, fretful.

Ted turned to Bill and spoke to him.

"Bill, I'm so sorry that I didn't have much time for you in the past, but I need your help with this."

"Since you just apologised, sure, why not?" Bill said, a little ambivalent.

"I will leave you both to get on with the task at hand. You must find the location of the lens. I will be observing you both and will return when you know the location. I will then take you back to correct this wrong," the strange being said.

"Wait, why can't *you* do this task? Why does it have to be us anyway?" asked Bill.

"I would be much too obvious, and I am not privy to the location of the lens. However, you both going about your daily activities shouldn't attract much attention, but they are now aware that something is not right."

With that response from the strange being, he was gone—puffed away.

Ted turned to Bill and noticed he was a little distressed. He realised there and then that chaos was something Bill was always experiencing, and it would never get any better.

"Bill, have you noticed anything strange in New Cedars before the Flash?"

"I am a paranoiac. I never go outside the door, particularly to avoid interacting with people like you—strange. I'm not even Bill Stravinsky, and you're not really Ted Malone, and yet we are behaving and thinking like them. The only thing I noticed as strange was when Mayor Kelly stole my idea for the clock tower. It must have been the aliens somehow reading my mind. Why should we care—we are what they would label—the *aliens* too."

"I know. We are aliens being used by aliens, and all I know is I can't face tomorrow unless things are put back in the right way. Wait! Did you just say the clock tower in the town hall?"

"Yeah, so. I told you Mayor Kelly planted a bug in my home, and when I first thought of it, I said it out loud."

Ted thought for a second. "It's funny. Just hours before the Flash, I noticed a strange light coming from the numerals: twelve, three, six, and nine. Come to think of it, the sunlight—it didn't seem natural, like it was synthetic, much like the light in the Afterglow. Could that be the lens?"

"There's only one way to find out. We gotta go up there."

One hour passed, and Ted got into Bill's old jeep. Ted hid with covers over him in the back as they made their way to the centre of the town. On the way, Bill thought he was being followed by the Sheriff but put this down to probable paranoia.

"I thought Sheriff Sears was following us, but I lost him."

They headed into the forest slowly.

"First, we got to check on Lorna and Adele. They're just two miles west of the forest."

They got back inside the jeep, Ted under the covers, and Bill drove to the cabin. When they arrived there, Ted quickly got out and knocked on the cabin's door. Lorna came out and gestured to Ted, who was just about to ask if they were both all right, to shush. Ted gestured in turn for Bill to go inside quietly.

Lorna spoke lowly and softly. "She's sleeping. Hi, Bill."

"Hello, Ma'am," Bill said, then turned to Ted. "How much does your wife know?"

"How much *is* there to know?" Lorna asked her husband.

"Look, it's late. Us two have to be going, but I want you to know, we're going to fix this."

Lorna was unsure whether to believe him and

was about to speak when they all heard Adele crying.

"I'd better check on her before I go," Ted said as he went toward her bedroom. He went inside and went over to comfort his daughter. "Don't worry, honey. It will be over soon." He kissed her head and headed back to his wife and Bill. To his shock, he saw Sheriff Sears standing there with two deputies.

"Ted Malone, please bring your daughter out to me, or I will get her by force!"

"She's not here. She is on the other side of town with her auntie!"

"Don't lie to me, Malone. Gentlemen!"

The two deputies went toward the bedroom, only to be pushed into each other by Ted. Sheriff Sears took out his gun and pointed it at Ted.

"I'm placing you under arrest." He continued to read him his rights when Adele came out slowly from her room.

"Daddy, I'm scared!" she cried.

Lorna went over to hold her daughter's hand while Bill urged Ted, "Ted, you have to give her up. It's the only way."

"No!" cried Lorna as they handcuffed him.

Ted watched helplessly as Sears brought his little girl to the police car. She was staring back at him, tears falling from her frightened eyes.

"Daddy, don't let them take me!"

The two deputies escorted Ted into another police car as Bill was starting up his jeep. He quickly drove into the police car and got out, grabbing one of the deputy's guns that had been flung across the ground. He picked it up and shot the two deputies. Ted got up as Bill took the handcuff keys from one of the deputies' pockets. He freed Ted.

Ted rushed over to Lorna.

"I'll make this right!"

"Just how on Earth are you gonna do that, tell me?"

Ted hadn't the answer to that question. "You must go home. Just trust me," he replied.

Bill drove Ted and Lorna back home. On their way, they noticed a bright light pulsating in the four-faced clock tower. Bill stopped the jeep, and they got out to take a look.

"He must be waiting for us," Ted said.

The strange being came closer to them, and the light followed him. "Good news. Phase One is complete. You all performed admirably, and now you can return with me back to our realm. Phase Two will commence shortly," he said to a bewildered Ted and Bill.

"No! You promised us that we got to return to our human bodies and prevent Phase Two!" Ted yelled at the strange being as he was moving away.

"None of you are human. Stop caring about

them. They are a selfish, stubborn, and destructive race."

As the strange being was preaching those words to Ted, Bill crept up beside the peculiar being, reached out his hand, and clenched a fist in the strange being's stomach as he transformed back into his energy state. The being yelled, "*Noooh!*" in a metallic-sounding voice. An energy beam shot out from Bill's chest. Ted moved in closer, realising that he had to touch the strange being too, and so he did, resulting in an energy beam shooting out from him also. These two beams, in turn, shot up toward the Afterglow, which began to scintillate with light.

Ted was back at his car hours before when the Afterglow first occurred. He listened out for the weird electrical sound, but there was none and nor was there a bright flash. He was back. He rushed into his car and found his penknife. He slowly cut the palm of his hand. It bled, and now he knew he was human.

Bill was outside the store to purchase cigars. He took a deep breath and sighed, "I'm back."

He quickly headed for the centre of town to find Ted. He was successful. When they were reunited, they smiled, but their euphoria was short-lived as it was about the time that Mayor Kelly was giving his speech on the reopening of the town hall. They waited until it concluded. Bill had the urge to spit but turned to Ted and found he was shaking his head in disapproval.

"We have to blow up that lens. If we don't, all this could begin again," Ted urged Bill.

Bill nodded in agreement.

It was evening now, and Ted and Bill had explosives that Ted had made. After all, he was a competent science teacher. Bill picked the lock of the door to the town hall, and they were now inside.

"Don't like what he did with the place," Bill complained.

"Come on, the door to the tower is not far."

They were now inside the tower, climbing the stairs to the top. They found two wooden doors sealing the clock. They pulled and pulled, with Bill almost falling down the stairs, but they managed to open them. Inside, it appeared to be a normal, standard clock tower mechanism.

"Where is the alien technology?" Bill asked.

"They must have it concealed. They're good. We'd better blow the whole thing up."

As he made that reply to Bill, Ted structured the explosives around the clock mechanism.

"It's done. We'd better get back down 'cause this is gonna blow," Ted urged Bill.

They made their way back down the tower's stairs and arrived back inside the town hall itself, only to find Mayor Kelly and Sheriff Sears waiting for them.

"Gentlemen, were you tampering with my clock?" the mayor asked.

"It's my clock!" Bill yelled.

"Sheriff Sears, after you lock up these two, throw that one in the nearest looney bin."

"We know you're both aliens!" Bill continued.

"That's it. I've heard enough," Sheriff Sears said as he cuffed Bill.

Ted didn't waste a second and pushed the remote button linked to the detonator. "We all have to get out now!" he said.

They all exited the town hall and ran. When they were a safe distance away, nothing happened.

"Sheriff Sears, I want you to release these men. It was just a charade. They were playing on me for the reopening. You got me," Mayor Kelly said to Sears.

"Oh, you had me going there. Gentlemen, nice joke."

Sears went back to his police car and drove away, while a flabbergasted Ted and Bill demanded an explanation. Mayor Kelly morphed into the strange being. "It appears that the human race has an excess of resolve. We are terminating our experiment as a result. You require much too counteractive cunning to combat your devious ways. We will move on. Goodbye."

The strange being morphed back into Mayor Kelly. "What's going on? How did I end up here?" he demanded.

Ted and Bill struggled for an explanation. "Ah, ah, you had too much to drink after the reopening party and wandered off," Ted said quickly.

"Nice design on the clock, by the way," Bill added.

"Let me get you home. Your wife is probably worried," Ted said as he helped Mayor Kelly to his car to give him a lift home.

Later on, as Bill was walking back to his home, he heard Ted's car pulling up. Ted yelled at him, "Guess we're back to being human beings again."

Ted pulled over and got out. "It looks like the aliens didn't count on how cunning human beings really are; otherwise, they would have begun the Afterglow experiment over again."

"I wouldn't count on it. They could go back to any time in our past and initiate it."

"Now, you're paranoid, Bill."

"Am I? When I was connected to that weird being, I gained access to their thoughts – if they ever really figure humanity out – they're planning it. We will never be safe."

"All I need to know is that I don't have to remember my little girl's face as they took her away for too long. But on the bright side, I suppose this means now that I'm going to be a granddad – Christopher and his girlfriend are expecting a baby."

"And you're not mad?"

"Ordinarily, I would be, but not now. Come and join us for dinner tonight, Bill?"

Bill shrugged. "Maybe tomorrow night. Right now, I've got some personal reflection to do."

Ted started up his car and drove home to be with his wife and all of his family.

THE END

ABOUT THE AUTHOR

 John Paul Warren was born on June 12, 1975 in Ireland. He writes passionately in his free time about characters who are pulled into ethical dilemmas and use personal introspection to solve their problems and usually references on our ever so strange human condition.

To learn more about John P. Warren and discover more Next Chapter authors, visit our website at www.nextchapter.pub.

Mesmerized
ISBN: 978-4-82412-537-8
Large Print

Published by
Next Chapter
2-5-6 SANNO
SANNO BRIDGE
143-0023 Ota-Ku, Tokyo
+818035793528

23rd December 2024

www.ingramcontent.com/pod-product-compliance
Lightning Source LLC
LaVergne TN
LVHW011046100526
838202LV00078B/3333